PIECES OF YOU

BOOK ONE: THE MISSING PIECES SERIES

N.R. WALKER

COPYRIGHT

BLURB

Missing Pieces Series, Book One.

Dallas Muller has everything he never expected he'd have. He owns a successful motorbike mechanic shop in Newcastle, and he's madly in love with his boyfriend of four years, Justin Keith.

Justin has always struggled to find where he fit in, never realising his true worth or what it means to be loved—until he met Dallas. Living and working together might be too much for some, but Dallas and Justin wouldn't have it any other way.

When a terrible accident tears their world apart, Justin's left with no memory of Dallas or their relationship. Trying to put the pieces back together is almost impossible when some pieces are blank and some are missing altogether. Dallas has to let Justin find his own way back to him and just hope that their love will light the way.

PIECES

OF

you

MISSING PIECES SERIES
BOOK ONE

CHAPTER ONE

JUSTIN

DALLAS SLID a mug of coffee on the kitchen bench in front of me. "You'll need to take the van today," he said, nodding to the overcast and dreary day.

I sighed. "Thanks," I mumbled before taking a sip. I was unsure if that order was coming from my boyfriend or my boss. Though that was probably unfair. Dallas was both boyfriend and boss, and we'd never had a problem with blurred lines before. I was just in a pissy mood.

I wasn't in a bad mood, exactly. I just wasn't a morning person. The rainy weather didn't help, considering I was a mobile bike mechanic, which meant I'd be working in the rain today. I loved my job, and I loved Dallas. I just didn't love mornings. Dallas squeezed my arm and fought a smile as he walked out of the kitchen.

I met Dallas when I was twenty-five. I'd not long moved back to Newcastle from two years in Darwin. The best motorbike mechanic shop in town was looking for a new mechanic, and I was a perfect fit for the job. They wanted a dedicated, hard-working KTM expert, and that's what they got. I was looking for work and certainly wasn't actively looking for a boyfriend, but along with the perfect job, I found a guy who was a perfect fit for me.

He was tall and gorgeous, with brown hair and a jawline of scruff and piercing hazel-grey eyes. He was also the strong and silent type who never said much. He was hard-working, strict but fair, and everyone respected him. He was also kind and gentle, had a quirky sense of humour, and would do anything to help anyone. It helped that we shared a passion for bikes and that neither of us minded grease-stained fingernails and the permanent smell of oil on our skin.

Being gay and a mechanic was hard enough. It never occurred to me to look twice at a guy at any shop I worked at. Typically, mechanic shop breakrooms had calendars of naked women and guys who bragged about scoreboards of bedrooms and weekend football.

But not Dallas, and not his shop. He was different. And when I first started working with him, I'd thought I'd imagined the way his gaze would linger just a beat too long or how he'd stop and smile . . . because there was no way—no freaking way—he could look at me like that.

I hadn't been there long when Davo, another mechanic and a good mate of Dallas' asked me if I had a girlfriend. I'd laughed it off, shaking my head, not wanting to give my sexuality away, but then he'd asked if I had a boyfriend.

I'd frozen, and somewhere in the workshop a spanner had hit the concrete floor.

"It's okay," Davo had said, smiling a little too much. "I mean, we're cool with it here. Aren't we, Dallas?"

I'd shot Dallas a look over where he was picking up his dropped spanner while I was trying not to freak out and wondering how best to deny everything.

"Course it's fine," Dallas had mumbled, glaring at Davo before turning back to the bike he was working on.

Davo had laughed and walked away, finding something amusing, and I had tried not to dwell on it. But I knew guys who'd been bullied or, worse, bashed at work when they'd been outed. That afternoon at knock-off time, I'd been cleaning up in the breakroom when Dallas had come in. I hadn't noticed everyone else was gone, but the shop looked deserted.

I'd thought for sure he was about to fire me. Or jump me and hold me down while everyone took turns in kicking the shit outta me. But he'd looked troubled, awkward even, had scratched his beard, and swallowed hard. "I uh . . ." He'd let out a breath. "I just want you to know that if you're gay, that it's okay. I mean . . ." He'd shook his head. "Jesus."

"I'm not," I'd lied.

"Because I am," he'd said at the same time. He'd stared at me. "Oh." He'd frowned, and I'd regretted seeing the hurt in his eyes.

"Oh, um... Shit," I'd stammered.

"You okay?" he'd asked, putting a hand on my shoulder. His hand was huge and so warm, it had burned through my overalls. "Wanna breathe for me?"

I remembered sucking back a breath, putting a hand to my forehead. "Yeah, thanks. I thought . . ."

He'd taken his hand back and leaned against the sink, casual as ever. "You thought what?"

"I mean, I'm out. People know . . . I'm gay, that is. I just don't advertise it, especially at work because sometimes . . ."

"Sometimes people are arseholes."

I'd nodded quickly. "Yeah. Was Davo . . . ?"

He'd grinned. "Davo's fine. He's a mate of mine. The guys here know, and hell, most of my clients too. They don't have a problem with me. Well, if they do, they're too chick-enshit to say anything."

I'd smiled at him and he'd stared that hazel-grey stare. My stomach had flipped, and he'd given me a crooked smile in return. And that was the beginning of months of too-long looks, shy smiles and off-the-charts sexual tension. Until Davo and Sparra called us into the breakroom and told us enough was enough. They were done with the tiptoeing and the breath-holding and how antsy I was and how pissed off Dallas was. "You're both not leaving this room until you sort it out," Davo had said, slamming the door behind him.

Dallas didn't want to have a relationship with a staff member, because lines got crossed, he'd said. I'd nodded because I understood, that made perfect sense, and I wasn't keen on shacking up with the boss either. He'd nodded and I'd nodded, and for a few long seconds, we'd stood, trying to breathe, like there was no oxygen in the room. He'd licked his lips, and holy shit, those eyes . . .

I'd taken one step closer before I even knew what I was doing, and he'd crossed the floor and had hold of my face and his tongue in my mouth before I could think.

But I didn't need to think . . .

Because I just knew.

"WHAT'S GOT YOU SMILING?" Dallas asked.

I was still staring out the rain-splattered window. "Just remembering our first kiss."

Dallas laughed and put his empty cup in the sink. "Fucking Davo. Still takes credit for that, you know."

"Oh, I know. He tells me all the time."

He stepped in close, lifted my jaw, and planted a soft

kiss on my lips. "And I still thank him." His phone buzzed and he groaned. "First one for the day."

It had just gone six-thirty. I nodded and took a mouthful of coffee. "Gonna be a day of it, I'd say."

He glanced to the weather outside the kitchen window and nodded. "I'll go restock the van."

"Be down in a sec." The 'commute to work' was a single flight of stairs because we lived in the flat above the mechanic shop. Well, Dallas owned the building, and that included his business and his home. It was a two-bedroom unit that wasn't about to win any fancy-living awards, but it suited us perfectly.

I finished my coffee and pulled on my boots, gave Squish the cat a scratch behind his ear, pocketed my phone and keys, and pulled the door locked behind me.

By ten to seven in the morning, I'd finished loading up the van with Dallas when he handed me his high-vis rain-coat. "Dunno if it'll keep you completely dry," he said as the rain poured down outside.

"If I come back soaking wet, will it be asking too much for the boss to get me out of my wet uniform? You know, being a work-safety thing and all."

Dallas gave me my favourite smirk. "Nah, the paper-work's a bitch."

My mouth fell open, making him laugh, and he gave me a quick kiss just as Davo ran into the shop with his coat pulled over his head.

"It's pissing down," he said. He pulled his coat off with a grin, then shook the water off himself like a dog.

Sparra followed in not far behind him, dripping wet. "Good weather for ducks, ay."

"Yeah, you lot have a really awful day here in the fully-enclosed, dry shop. I've already got a call out," I said, holding up my PalmPilot.

"Uh, make that two," Dallas said, looking at his phone. He thumbed something on the screen, then the second booking popped up on my screen.

"Great," I grumbled. "You lot enjoy your second cuppa. I'll be out in that." I nodded toward the deluge blowing in through the open roller door.

Davo and Sparra laughed and flipped me off as they disappeared into the breakroom. Dallas shook his head, smiling. He fixed the collar of my coat and kissed me. "Be careful."

"Always."

He smirked at the rain. "I'll, uh, I'll have the report filled out by the time you get back."

"Report?"

"For the wet clothes," he murmured, his voice full of gravel and promise.

I laughed as I got into the van. First stop was Glendale, so it wasn't far, maybe fifteen minutes tops with this rain. I put the wipers on full bore, cranked the heater up so the windscreen didn't fog up, and hit the road.

It was supposed to be just another ordinary Tuesday in a very ordinary life. A day of work, some laughs with the boys at the shop in the afternoon, maybe a jog after work. Or if this rain hung around, maybe Dallas and I would curl up on the couch with Squish and watch some TV, then fall into bed and make real slow love till late.

Completely ordinary, completely mundane, and completely wonderful. It was all I'd ever wanted and never dared dream to have. Until I met Dallas and he made every wrong in my life right. It was ridiculous how happy I was.

Even when I woke up grumpy in the mornings, he still smiled at me and he still loved me, no matter what.

Life was damn near perfect. Actually, there wasn't one single thing I would change if I was given the chance. Not one thing.

I sat in a line of traffic waiting for the lights to turn green. The rain had eased a little, though the taillights in front of me were still refracted by the water and the lights. Cold Chisel came on the radio, so I turned the volume up and began to sing along to "When the War Is Over." Dallas and I didn't exactly have a song, but if we did, this would be it. A song about learning to live again; a true classic Aussie anthem about life.

Life . . .

It's funny how they say your life flashes before your eyes just before you die. Or that there is profound clarity the moment before your life ends.

I had none of that.

As I was following the slow line of traffic through the intersection, the light still green, and just when Jimmy Barnes was about to belt out his part of the song, I heard the sound of screeching brakes and honking horns. I just happened to look out my window at the truck aquaplaning straight for me. It was jack-knifed and sliding and coming so fast and in slow motion at the same time.

No, there was no life flashing before my eyes, no profound moments of clarity. As the grille of the truck came at me, my very last thought would have been funny if it hadn't been my very last thought.

Oh, that's just fucking great. The song's just getting to my favourite part.

I waited for the sound of impact, to hear the breaking

glass and twisting metal. I waited for the pain. But it never came.

CHAPTER TWO

DALLAS

I CHECKED the clock at ten to nine. Two minutes since I checked it last. Justin hadn't checked in yet, and he always checked in. His first job should've been finished ages ago.

"He'll be fine," Davo said, catching me clock-watching for the twentieth time. We'd been working on a bike together at the far end of the shop. "He'll drive in any second now lookin' like a drowned rat, bitching about the rain. You watch."

"Hmm," I grunted, not feeling his confidence.

"Uh, Dallas? Boss," Sparra called out with an edge to his voice.

Davo and I turned just as two uniformed officers walked in. My blood ran cold and my stomach soured. "Can I help you?" I asked.

"This is Forty-four Carney Road?" one of the officers asked.

"Yes, that's right."

The other officer spoke. "We have this as the address of a Mr Justin Keith."

My knees almost buckled. "That's right. He lives upstairs with me." I swallowed hard and my lungs felt far too small.

"You're Dallas Muller?"

"Yeah, that's right." I was trying real hard not to freak out. "I'm his boyfriend. And his boss. We live together. Is everything okay?"

Maybe it was my tone or the flat-out panic in my voice, but the first cop took pity on me. "There's been an accident, Mr Muller. We're going to need you to come with us."

Accident.

"Is he . . . ?" Fuck. No, they didn't take their hats off. Cops take their hats off if it's real bad news, right?

"He's been taken to John Hunter. The vehicle he was driving was T-boned by a truck."

I didn't hear much after that. My legs didn't want to hold me up anymore and the air got real thick and heavy . . .

I remember seeing the look of horror on Davo and Sparra's faces. Davo took my keys, told me he'd look after the shop, and helped me get into the cop car. I don't remember the drive to the hospital. I just remember trying not to vomit. And trying to breathe.

The two officers escorted me straight through the emergency department and I found myself in a waiting room. The foul hospital smell clung to the back of my throat, and one cop handed me a plastic cup of water with a look of pity and the other cop came back with a woman in scrubs.

"This is Dallas Muller. He's the boss *and* boyfriend of the patient from the vehicle accident."

"His name's Justin Keith. We live together," I said numbly.

She looked at me, at my dirty overalls and my grease-covered hands. "Does he have any family?"

Oh fuck.

"Um, not really. His mother doesn't care about him," I whispered. "His sister lives in Sydney. I can try to get her number. It'd be in Justin's phone, in the van, maybe. He had his phone with him when he left this morning. Is he okay? Please . . ."

She didn't answer. "Does he have any allergies?"

"Uh, no. I don't think so." My hands began to shake and my eyes burned. "I'm sorry, this is all a bit much to take in. Where is he? Can I see him? Please. Please."

She had weary eyes, I noticed. She put her hand on my arm. "Mr Muller, he's in surgery. His right arm is broken, and he has multiple fractures in his right leg . . ."

I nodded. "Okay." Arms and legs were okay. They could be fixed, more or less.

"Mr Muller, there was also some head trauma. I don't know the extent and I won't speculate, but he's in the best hands right now."

I didn't hear much after that. There was something about MRI and CT scans and something else about not knowing for a few hours yet, but the room began to pulse and spin and the nice officers sat me back in a chair. Even they left after a while, and hospital staff came and went, but I sat in that waiting room for I don't know how long. The chair was probably uncomfortable but I never felt a thing.

An eternity later and Davo and Sparra arrived, peering cautiously around the wall. "Oh, there you are," Davo said. "They said you were up here . . ." His frown deepened. "What do you know?"

"Nothing much," I answered, my voice sounding rough. "He has a broken arm and leg, and there's some head trauma. He's in surgery. He's been in surgery for fucking hours."

Sparra handed me my phone. "You left that at work."

"Thanks, mate."

"I know it's a bit early but we were so worried. I locked everything up and fed Squish," Davo said. "And don't you worry about nothin', Dallas. I'll open up in the morning and take care of everything. You just worry about him, 'kay?"

I nodded, overwhelmed with gratitude for these two and fear for my Justin. I swallowed back tears. "What time is it?" I asked as I checked my phone. Shit. It was after two o'clock in the afternoon.

"The accident's been on the news and everything," Davo said gently. "There are photos of the van. Fuck, Dallas. It don't look good. They're saying it's a miracle he survived."

I stared at the black screen on my phone, not daring to see any news, any reports, or pictures. My heart couldn't bear it. "He got hit by a truck."

Davo nodded, his mouth a thin line, his eyes full of sorrow. "It went through a red light. The brakes locked up, apparently, and it just slid right into him. There was nothing Justin coulda done."

I shook my head, feeling all kinds of hollowed out. "Fuck."

Just then, a doctor came in, and when he saw us, three rough-looking mechanics, he smiled. "Mr Muller?"

I stood, and Davo and Sparra stood beside me. "Yeah, that's me. How is he, doc? Is he okay?"

His smile died, but there was kindness in his eyes. "He came through the surgery and they're taking him through to recovery."

My breath left me in a whoosh and I almost sagged with relief. "Thank fuck." Sparra patted my back, and I willed myself not to cry.

"He's not out of the woods yet," the doc said firmly. "In fact, we won't know the extent of his injuries until he wakes up. He took quite a blow, the impact resulting in a subdural haematoma. We operated to relieve the bleed and the pressure. His arm has been reset, but his leg will require some surgery, though our main concern right now is his brain. They won't operate on his leg until his brain injury is stabilised. There is some swelling, which we're monitoring, but Mr Muller, brain injuries are complex. There can be lasting damage that may affect him for the rest of his life. We won't know the extent until he wakes up."

I nodded, still numb. "But he survived. Everything else we can live with."

He gave me a sympathetic smile, and I didn't know if he pitied my naivety or if he liked my optimism. But I had to believe Justin would be okay.

He just had to be. Because the alternative was incomprehensible.

"Can I see him? Please?"

The doc gave a nod. "Just for a minute. He won't be awake for some time, so a quick visit. Then you might as well go home and get some rest yourself."

"I'm not leaving," I replied. Wild fucking horses . . .

He gave a nod like he expected me to say exactly that. "Come with me." He shot a glance to Davo and Sparra. "He'll be a few minutes if you want to wait here."

They both nodded, and I followed the doc through the double doors and down the hall. He stopped near a blue curtain. "He'll be in Intensive Care at first," the doc said, his voice low. "But I'll see you tomorrow and hopefully we'll know a lot more."

The doc was gone then, and a nurse took his place. She pulled back the curtain and I almost couldn't look.

Jesus, how did this even happen? How did he leave just this morning, smiling as he bitched about the rain, and now here he was in hospital?

It felt so surreal.

Until I saw him.

He was bandaged . . . everywhere: his arm, his head. He had tubes and so many monitors, and his face—God, what I could see of it—was banged up and bruised. He looked far too pale and there was dried blood smeared . . .

Christ almighty, nothing in the world could have prepared me for seeing him like that.

He was impossibly still, and Justin was never still . . .

The nurse put her hand on my arm. "Two minutes. Then we're taking him to the ICU."

I nodded, I think. I couldn't seem to move. My feet felt welded to the floor. I had to make myself move closer, mechanically and heavy, to the left side of the bed. I reached for his hand, though it had tubes taped to it. It was cold and it didn't feel like him at all. I held his fingers, and it took me a second to realise why it felt so foreign.

Because he never threaded our fingers like he always did. He never moved to touch me back like he always did. Even in his sleep, as soon as he felt me near, he would curl into me or squeeze me.

But this time he never moved.

Hot tears spilled and I sobbed back a breath. "Justin, baby. It's me. You're gonna be okay. I'm here."

The right side of his body had obviously taken the brunt of the hit. His arm was wrapped from his shoulder to his fingers, the bedding was held off his right leg; I was grateful I couldn't see it. And though his head was bandaged, I could see his right eye was swollen, and there looked to be stitches above his eyebrow. His cheek was purple, his jaw marked, and he had small cuts and nicks all over, from the shattered glass, I guessed.

The left side of his face wasn't so banged up, but his eyelid was purple. His beautiful eyelashes fanned out, casting delicate shadows on his pale cheek. A cheek I'd touched a thousand times.

He was so still.

The nurse appeared at my side. "I'm sorry. Time's up. We need to take him."

"I just got here. It's not two minutes yet."

She gave me a curt smile. "Rasida will show you out. You can see him again in the ICU after three o'clock."

I didn't even have time to argue because a swarm of scrubs came in and wheeled Justin away. A short woman with a kind face smiled up at me. "Come with me," she said, leading me back the way I'd come. "I know it's scary right now, but they're taking him where he needs to be." She continued to talk in a smooth, calming tone as we walked, not that I heard much of anything. Then we were back in the waiting room and Davo and Sparra both shot to their feet when they saw me.

"Ah," Rasida said. "Get him something to eat and a juice or a soft drink. He can come down to the ICU after three o'clock." She held up three fingers, then patted me on the back but spoke to Davo. "You take him now."

They nodded and she left, and then they looked up at me. "Is he . . . ?" Davo started. "How was he?"

I shook my head, not able to speak. My eyes burned and a tear escaped, but I quickly scrubbed it away. "He doesn't look too good," I tried to say.

Sparra squeezed my shoulder. "He's not the only one. Come on, she said to feed you."

I put my hand to my stomach. The thought of food

made me nauseous. "I just need to sit down," I said, my voice still not working right.

I found myself sitting in a chair trying to take deep breaths. Sparra was gone, but Davo was beside me, his expression grave. I had to tell him something. "The whole right side of his body took the worst of it," I managed. "He looked dead. I thought he was dead."

"He'll get better," Davo said, patting me gently on the back. "You know how stubborn he is. He's too pigheaded to die."

I laughed, though it sounded more like a sob. I wiped my face. "He sure is stubborn."

Sparra appeared then, holding a packet of rice crackers and a can of lemonade. "Found a vending machine," he said, holding them out to me. I tried to wave him off because the last thing I wanted to do was eat. "Boss," Sparra said. "You look green. If you want to see Justin again today, you need to not be sick. They won't let you near him if you're fucking green. Now eat."

I stared up at him in shock, and Davo did too, until he laughed.

"What I mean to say," Sparra added, "is that you probably should eat something, please. That doctor-lady said you should too. So here."

He was still holding them in front of me, so I took them. I had to sip the lemonade to wash the cracker down, but after the first stayed down, I had a few more and half the lemonade, and I did feel a bit better.

Davo stood up. "Come on," he said, nodding for me to stand. "It's almost three. You can see him again soon."

"I don't know where the ICU is," I admitted as I got to my feet. At least my knees weren't so wobbly now.

Sparra stood with me. "Then we'll find it."

Ten minutes later, I stood outside the ICU. "Don't worry about the shop," Davo said. "We got it covered. You just concentrate on him."

"Yeah, and tell him to hurry and get his lazy arse back to work," Sparra added with a smile. Then he nodded, more serious. "And you tell him to get better soon, 'kay?"

I gave a nod. "Thanks, guys."

I went through the door and was met by a clerk who threw twenty rapid-fire questions at me. No, I wasn't family. I was his de facto. We live together. Yes, boyfriends. Next of kin, his normal doctor, private health insurance details, Medicare info, sign here . . .

"I just need to see him," I said and was eventually, after an eternity, taken to one nurse in particular.

"Ah, you're his partner," she said warmly. She walked me to bed five. "He's all settled in for now. You can hold his hand, talk to him."

She didn't have to tell me to be quiet. The room was like a tomb. It was cold and there was nothing but the sound of beeps and respirators, and I didn't dare look at any of the other beds. I just sat by his side and took his hand. I marvelled at how our hands matched: rough, calloused, our oil-and-grease-stained nails. We each had cuts and bumps on our fingers. These hands worked hard for our money, but they also loved and caressed and touched . . . I knew his hands, how they felt on my body, how he loved to hold hands . . . I brought his knuckles up to my lips, closed my eyes, and cried.

TWO DAYS later—two days of nothing but sympathetic

looks from doctors and nurses, two days of listening to every beep, every blip, every heartbeat, when hope was starting to fade—Justin opened his eyes.

CHAPTER THREE

"HEY," I whispered, real low. My voice croaked from disuse.

Justin's left eye closed, then half opened again. His right eye was still swollen shut, but this was the first sign of life in two days. Surely it meant he was waking up.

"Hey," I tried again. "You're okay. You're in hospital. I'm right here, baby."

His eyelid slowly closed again and, this time, stayed closed. His nurse today was Naomi, and she was quick to check all the machines he was hooked up to and write everything down. She smiled at me. "Could be a good sign."

Could be?

"I'm sure it is," I said, touching the side of Justin's face. "If you need to sleep, baby, you take all the time you need. I'm not going anywhere."

Naomi did something to the machines and took a printout of some kind with Justin's folder. "Keep talking to him," she said.

"Talk to him? About what?"

"It doesn't matter. Just keep it nice and calm. I'm sure

he likes the sound of your voice."

I sat back down and took his hand again. I wasn't game to take my eyes off his in case he opened them. "Uh, so I called your sister. She's gonna come up next weekend," I began. "She texts me for updates every day. I think she told your mum. I'm not sure though. Hopefully it might make your mother pull her head out of her arse."

Naomi quirked an eyebrow at me and smiled. "Sorry. I didn't mean to hear that."

"It's okay. His mother's . . . not very nice."

"Lucky he has you," she said with a wink before heading back to the nurses' station.

"Of course he has me," I whispered to Justin. I stared at his face, his beautiful, bandaged and swollen face. "They've done more scans on your brain and they're happy there's no more bleeding, and the swelling's gone down but there's still some bruising. Doc said he's still not sure of what effect the extent of the damage will have on ya, but he did say you'll have a cracker of a headache for a long while. He's one of the best brain doctors in the country, apparently, so he knows his stuff. He said brains are complex and delicate, and yours took a helluva hit. There was a fracture in your skull and a bleed that shut off some blood to one part of your brain."

I was just rambling, all out of order, trying to remember everything they'd told me. "Your arm was broken up near your shoulder and in your forearm. They told me the name of the bones, but I can't remember it. The one near your elbow, is that the radius? I dunno what they called it." I squeezed his hand. "Your leg isn't too good, but nothing they can't fix. They just want to worry about your head first. Your leg'll need surgery, apparently. They must have you on some pretty good drugs if you can't feel it. But they said maybe an operation tomorrow, depends how you fare today. They're more worried about your head than your leg." I kissed his knuckles. "Just one day at a time, baby. That's all you can do."

I didn't tell him that the doctor had said he might never fully recover or that he might have some permanent brain damage. Or that he might have lost the ability to speak or walk properly. Or that we had to face the possibility that his life would never be the same. He might need a full-time carer; he would likely need all kinds of therapy for years. He might never regain consciousness.

Except he just did. For a fleeting moment, his eye opened. He was still in there. I knew it.

I knew it was the doctor's responsibility to prepare people for the worst. I understood why. But I was ready for the worst. Whatever issues we had to face, we'd face together.

I kissed Justin's hand again and held his fingers to my cheek, closed my eyes, and sighed. Together forever, I repeated to myself. Together forever.

I took a moment and began again. "Anyway, Davo and Sparra have been a godsend, if you can believe that. I mean, they've always been good blokes, but they've really stepped up and looked after the shop for us. I haven't been to work at all. You were always saying I needed to take some time off." I couldn't even smile. "Davo's been taking care of everything. I only go home to shower and sleep. Pretty sure the nurses here are sick of my face. Squish misses you too. Not as much as me, of course. I know I bitched a lot about you hogging the blankets, but Justin, I'd do anything to have you back in our bed. I miss you so much. So any time you want to open those pretty eyes, you just go right ahead."

Justin's doctor appeared with Naomi at his side. "I hear

someone opened his eyes."

I nodded. "Just for a second. He blinked, real slow. But that's good news, right?"

He smiled and walked to the other side of the bed. He leaned over Justin and lifted his eyelid, peering into his eye with a penlight. "It can be, yes," he said.

"I mean, it's a sign that there's something going on in there, isn't it?"

The doctor gave me one of those patronising I-can't-say-because-I-don't-want-to-get-sued smiles. "We're still taking it one day at a time. His vitals are good. He's strong and healthy."

I sighed at his noncommittal reply, and after he finished looking at screens and printouts, I wasn't disappointed when he left.

The next day, Justin opened his eyes again. This time he kept them open for a few seconds. He didn't seem to focus on anything, and I tried to keep him with me. "Justin," I said, getting to my feet. I held his hand. "Hey, it's me, Dallas. You're okay. I'm right here."

His eyes closed slowly again and he slipped back to the comfort behind his eyelids.

The day after that, the nurse told me he'd opened his eyes a few times during the night, and I took my usual seat beside him and held his hand with a smile.

With hope.

I spent the morning reading to him, just page after page of quiet, soothing words. I even read the article on the new and improved Yamaha, which he would have hated, and maybe part of me wanted him to wake up just to tell me that KTMs were a better bike. It was an argument we'd had a thousand times, and truth be told, I probably would have agreed with him if the playful bickering wasn't so much fun.

"Whatcha reading to him?" Naomi asked as she pressed buttons on a screen.

I held it up so she could see the cover. "It's just the monthly motorbike magazine he subscribes to," I replied.

She grinned. "That's sweet."

Then Justin squeezed my fingers. "He squeezed my hand," I blurted. And when I looked over, his eyes were open. Still heavy-lidded but open, and more focused. "Hey," I whispered. "Justin, you're okay. You're in hospital. I'm right here beside you."

He blinked, and I thought his eyes would stay shut. But they opened again.

"I'll go page the doctor," Naomi said.

"You were in a bad car accident," I said. "But you're gonna be okay." I didn't know if that was the truth, but I wanted to reassure him any way I could.

He opened his mouth but no sound came out, then he slow blinked again. His eyes focused on me, but they were hazy, distant. He slow blinked another time, but on the next blink, his eyes stayed closed.

Forty minutes later, he opened them again. He seemed to focus better and was more alert. He opened and closed his mouth again. "Justin, can you hear me?" I asked. I stood and leaned over him so he could see me. "You're okay. You're in the hospital."

This time, his doctor and Naomi both arrived and there was another doctor with them as well. They took over and I stood aside, letting them do their thing. All the while, my heart was in my throat.

They asked him questions, not that he answered in words—he mostly grunted and squinted—but they were clearly happy with this development. This was progress. No matter how small.

23

Then Naomi was in front of me. "Okay, we're going to be taking him down for more scans and tests. It's almost rest time anyway, so why don't you come back after three."

"Oh, sure. Okay." I nodded, though I certainly didn't feel like leaving him. I checked my phone. It was almost midday, and rest time was one till three. Three hours . . . What the hell was I supposed to do for three hours?

Naomi patted my arm, clearly seeing me struggle. "Go home. Get something to eat. Have a nap. You've been here more hours than me this week, and that's saying something." She smiled. "We'll take good care of him."

So that's what I did. I went back to the shop, happier than I'd been in five days. I walked in carrying a bag of burgers and chips from the old takeaway shop a few blocks down.

Davo grinned when he saw me. He left the bike he was working on and stood in the middle of the doorway. "That smile has to mean good news."

"He opened his eyes."

"Well, I'll be fucking damned." He turned and yelled into the shop. "Hey, Sparra. Jusso opened his eyes!"

I held the bag up. "I bought us some lunch."

It felt good to smile again. After what had been the week from hell, I was beginning to wonder if I'd ever smile again. But there in the winter sunshine, sitting around with Davo and Sparra, listening to them talking shit and laughing, it was cathartic. Justin was in the best hands he could be in, and I fully expected to get back to the hospital at three o'clock and hear good news.

And I was smiling when I walked back through the ICU doors. I wanted to hold Justin's hand, look him right in the eye, and reassure him he was gonna be fine.

Except I didn't get the chance. Justin's curtains were

drawn and his doctor met me at the station. "Mr Muller," he said, his face unreadable. "I'd like to go somewhere to chat in private."

And I knew then, why he'd never said that Justin waking up was a good thing, why he never liked to give hope prematurely.

Because sometimes hope was the wrong thing to give.

He sat me down in a small room with awful yellow walls. My blood was pounding in my ears and my stomach was bubbling. Then he got straight to the point. "Mr Muller, when did Justin live in Darwin?"

"Darwin?" I shook my head. "Uh, like five years ago. He's from here originally. Went to Darwin for a few years but moved back to Newcastle five years ago. Why?"

"Hmm, five years . . ." He nodded like that made sense, but then his brows furrowed. "Have you heard of retrograde amnesia?"

"Amnesia? Like in the movies?"

There was that smile again . . . "I'm afraid it's not much like the movies at all. Unfortunately, it's not that simple."

"Is he talking? Does he not remember who he is?"

"He is talking, yes. Mostly just yes and no, which is a good sign, cognitively. There was no way to know just how much damage had been done or if he would be able to speak at all."

Okay, well, that was good, right? But amnesia? "I thought amnesia was not knowing who you are," I said, and as soon as I heard the words out loud, the penny dropped. "Oh."

The doctor nodded. "Justin remembers who he is. But he thinks he lives in Darwin. He believes he's twenty-five." He frowned. "Mr Muller, there's no easy way to say this. He doesn't know who you are."

CHAPTER FOUR

JUSTIN WAS SLEEPING when I went back into the ICU, and I was kind of glad. The hope I'd felt earlier was long gone, and in its place was a hollowed lump of dread.

The doctor said it could be temporary. Most cases saw a marked improvement in the days and weeks and months after the initial trauma. But he made it very clear that sometimes the memories never returned.

"The only true test is time," he'd said.

He'd begun to tell me other things, like what to expect and what it all meant, but I think he knew it was too much. I'd zoned out.

He doesn't know who you are.

He doesn't know who you are.

I sat by his bed and took his hand. It was warm in mine and I threaded our fingers, relishing in what might be the last time I held his hand for God knew how long—if ever. He was asleep, so I told myself it was to comfort him in his dreams, but I knew all too well it was for my benefit, not his.

And I told myself that it'd be okay. That his memory would come back in a day or two and we could concentrate on getting him better. That he'd remember me, and he'd remember us. I had to believe that. It wasn't hope. It was survival. Because he was my entire world. There was simply no other option.

I wouldn't give up on him.

I don't know how long I sat there like that, for minutes or hours. But he groaned and his eyelids slowly opened. He swallowed and groaned again, and I could only assume he was more with it because it sounded as though he was feeling every injury. Even with the drugs they were giving him.

He turned to me, and those beautiful, familiar eyes met mine. Those eyes that had shone when we'd laughed and burned when we'd made love. And now there was nothing . . .

No recognition, no spark. Only exhaustion and wariness.

He pulled his hand from mine. I'd forgotten I was holding it.

"Hey," I said weakly, trying not to let the hurt show. "I'm glad you're awake."

He slow blinked again and his lips parted, and his mouth worked like he was thirsty.

"Would you like some water?"

He hummed and gave a small nod, which made him wince.

"Naomi?" I said, going to the nurses' station. "Can he have water? I think he's thirsty."

She inclined his bed so he was sitting up a bit and gave him small sips of water, and he sagged back on the bed with another groan. He licked his lips and blinked, all in slow motion.

"Head hurts," he rasped slowly.

"You were in a car accident," I said. I wasn't sure what I should be telling him . . .

He frowned. He looked so different sitting up. His head was still bandaged across his right temple and the corner of his right eye, though the eye was still swollen shut. It was now purple and black, with mottled red splotches. The angry red mark on the right side of his jaw was still visible under his scruffy beard. His left eye was bruised and there was a cut across the bridge of his nose.

He looked like fucking hell.

And I hadn't seen the wound underneath those bandages yet. The doc had described what he'd done, so I could only imagine it, and it was no wonder his head hurt.

His right arm was still bandaged from his wrist to his armpit, and his leg was still broken. They'd stabilised it, of course, but they wouldn't risk surgery until they knew more about his brain activity.

"Head hurts," he said like he hadn't just said that. His words were a slow drawl.

"Would you like me to get the doctor?"

"Hmm." He slow blinked again, then his eyes drew to me. They were flat, empty, and confused. "You the doctor?"

My heart squeezed to the point of pain, and it was so sharp, the pierce of it took my breath away.

Naomi intervened, stepping in front of me and pulling the blanket up across his belly. "The doctor will be here soon," she said smoothly.

There was a long pause. "Head hurts," he mumbled.

"I know. We'll lie you back down now and you can close your eyes. That will help. Want another sip of water?" she asked, putting the cup to his lips. He sipped the drink without lifting his good hand, and his eyelids drooped heavily. He was asleep again before Naomi got the bed fully reclined.

She fixed his blanket again, then turned to me. "He's very confused, and that's to be expected." She put her hand on my arm and met my gaze. "Don't take it personally. I know that's easier said than done, but he doesn't mean it. Sit with him while he sleeps."

I nodded, numb, except for the burn behind my eyes.

But I sat, and he slept.

THEY OPERATED on Justin's leg the next day and they moved him to the neuro ward the day after that. He slept for most of it and would wake up and say that his head hurt. I would offer him sips of water and put the cup to his lips, and he would look at me with the same blank stare he gave the nurses and doctors. There was zero recognition.

They changed his head bandages and I saw the scars and staples for the first time. The side of his head was shaved, and there was an L-shape of staples from his temple down the back of his head. He had stitches above his eyebrow, which looked minor compared to the whopping surgical scar on the side of his head. His right eye was still badly bruised, but the swelling was starting to go down.

I fed him some beef broth, of which he managed just a few mouthfuls, but at least it was something. "Have you had enough?" I asked.

"Yeah," he murmured. "Thanks, doc."

I almost dropped the spoon, and my heart broke into a thousand tiny pieces.

TIME SEEMED to pass in a weird void. I had no idea if it was fast or slow. The only hours I kept were visiting hours. That's all there was. He was getting better, apparently, but he kept calling me doc. It broke my heart every time.

The thing about the neuro ward, as opposed to the ICU, was that he could have other visitors. And I'd just finished pushing the over-the-bed table away when Davo and Sparra arrived. They were escorted by a nurse who told them they had five minutes only.

They'd both showered after work, looking all kinds of nervous. And then they saw Justin.

Davo paled and Sparra took a small step back. "Oh," Davo said. "Thought we'd come visit." He looked at me, then, with a panicked look in his eyes. "He's, um . . ."

Justin looked at them, then looked at me. He was squinting again, a sign I now recognised as pain. "Can lights off, doc? Hurts m' eyes."

"Sure thing," I replied. I flipped the switch above his bed and he closed his eyes, quickly falling into sleep.

Davo and Sparra both stared at me, so I gave them a nod. "Wanna go for a walk? He'll be out for a while now."

They nodded woodenly, and both gave Justin a cautious once over before I led them out. I made it to the waiting room before I took a breath. "Holy shit," Davo said. "He looks . . ."

"Like he got hit by a truck?" I offered, trying to smile. I was also fighting tears. "He thinks I'm a doctor. Which is pretty cool, right? Means I look smart."

"Fuck," Sparra whispered. "Dallas, I'm sorry, man."

Davo nodded. "We thought we'd just come and visit him. Sorry. I shoulda checked first."

"No, you should visit. You're mates of his. He won't remember you now, but he might remember that you visited. Later on, in a coupla weeks or whatever. He'll remember that you came to see him."

"How you holding up?" Davo asked quietly. "We haven't seen ya since the other day, and it was good news back then . . ."

"I'm okay. I should have called or texted. Sorry. I've just been here. And I can't deal with much else right now. I've just dumped the shop onto you both. Sorry."

"Hey, it's okay. We got it all under control," Davo said. "Don't worry 'bout nothing. I put your mail on your desk though; you might wanna get that in case there's something important."

I nodded.

"Everyone knows about Justin," Sparra offered gently. "All the customers. They've been calling. And they all said to tell him to get better soon."

I managed a teary smile. "That's real nice."

"How long since you ate last?" Davo said, studying my face. He didn't need an answer. "Come on, let's go find the cafeteria."

A toasted sandwich and a cup of tea later, I felt somewhat better, though exhaustion started to catch up with me. I hadn't been sleeping well, at all. I'd tossed and turned all night, hugging his pillow in our very empty bed.

"So what'd the doc say?" Davo asked.

"He's got two plates and a bunch of pins in his leg, nineteen staples in his head, six stitches." I swallowed hard. "He, uh, thinks he's twenty-five and still living in Darwin."

"Fuck," Sparra breathed.

"The neurosurgeon said there was damage to the memory bank of his brain, and there's no way of knowing yet how bad it is. If he'll ever remember again, or even if he can even make new memories yet. Things like the name of his nurse, or if he just ate." I shrugged. "It's early days. And he sleeps a lot. Apparently that's common with a brain injury. I have a lot of information they've given me about what to expect. Things like exhaustion, real bad headaches, temper, confusion, anger. But he could remember everything when he wakes up tomorrow. Or next week. Or it could come to him in dribs and drabs over the next few weeks or months." *Or not at all . . .* I sighed then and tried to speak with a conviction I just didn't feel. "I mean, they weren't even sure if he'd be able to speak or communicate at all, and he's doing that just fine."

Davo shook his head sadly, but then he met my gaze with determination. "He'll be just fine. You watch. It might take a little while, but like I said, he's too stubborn to let a fucking truck stop him."

Sparra nodded. "Yep. And I know Jusso will do everything he can to make you happy. He'll come back to you, Dallas. His brain might have forgot, but this in here—" He thumped his heart. "It won't forget."

And with that, the tears I'd been trying not to cry fell like rain.

I ARRIVED AT THE HOSPITAL, just like every day since the accident, the second they opened the doors to visitors. Justin was sitting up in his bed surrounded by three doctors in white coats. His neurosurgeon, Doctor Anderson, smiled at me, though I had no idea who the other two were.

"Morning, Mr Muller," Doctor Anderson said. "These are Doctors Simeon and Chang. Justin's going to start some physiotherapy today with Doctor Simeon, and Doctor Chang is a cognitive recognition specialist. You'll be seeing more of them and less of me now going forward. They'll both need to speak with you at some point."

I gave them a nod, but honestly, I just wanted to see Justin.

"Hey," Justin said. "I know you."

And my heart stopped. Hope ignited like a forest fire in my chest. "You do?"

He smiled, slow and hazy. "Yeah. You were here before."

"I was, that's right." Come on, Juss. One more step. One more step . . .

"Are you a doctor?" he asked.

My heart sank, and I couldn't bring myself to speak.

Doctor Anderson stepped up, though I didn't hear what he said.

Doctor Chang led me toward the nurses' station, out of earshot. "That was rough for you," she said kindly. "I'd like to say it gets easier, but I'm not sure it does."

I shook my head, unsure of what to say to that and feeling very overwhelmed.

"My name is Julia Chang," she said. "I work with people who live with amnesia, and with their families and loved ones, helping to navigate the effects of traumatic brain injury. I'll be working with Justin, and you, from now on as he moves to the next stage of his recovery."

"Okay."

"Doctor Anderson said Justin has no close family and you'll be his primary carer? Is that correct?"

"Yes."

"I'll be working with Justin today to try and establish the extent of his amnesia, and I want you to be there. Do you think you can do that?"

"Yes."

"It won't be easy, and he may say things that are upsetting to hear."

"Like when he keeps calling me his doctor?"

Her eyes softened. "But he recognised you today from yesterday, and that is a good sign." She smiled. "That tells me he has the ability to make new memories, and that is very good news."

Of course it was. I knew it was. I was just still hurting over the doctor comment. "Okay."

"But first, we need to establish a basis from which to move forward. What we tell him as fact will be the foundation from which he can start."

I frowned. "I don't know what you mean."

"We cannot plant memories in his mind. It is best if he can remember on his own. But if he asks questions, we need to be honest in the facts without giving him our own opinions and experiences. It's not as easy as it sounds," she said. "Retrograde amnesia is the loss of facts and experiences but not the skill or the ability. He's a motorbike mechanic, yes?"

I nodded. "Yes."

"Right, so he won't remember if he owns a motorbike or when he bought. But he will remember how to ride it."

My mind was beginning to spin. "Okay."

"And we need to be united in what we tell him. He will begin to feel very overwhelmed and very lost and confused. We need to give him information he can anchor to, okay?"

"Such as."

"Things like where he lives, where he works. Who he's in a relationship with."

"Oh . . . I didn't think I could tell him that. I didn't want him to freak out . . ."

"We need to tell him this truth and show him photographs, or videos if you have them." She frowned but gave a nod. "If you were married, we would tell him without question. The fact you live together and he has no one else makes this case unusual. If we do not tell him in hopes he remembers on his own, yet he goes to live with you, it just raises more questions, more confusion, and untruths and lies. And that would be detrimental to his recovery and to his trust. Trust is critical here, so we must tell him the truth." Her eyes bored into mine. "But Mr Muller, you should prepare yourself . . . he may reject the idea, of you, of your relationship. You will need to give him all the space he needs, and you cannot pressure him. It will not be easy for either of you. Hard and sad for you, but terrifying and confusing for him."

I swallowed hard. "Okay."

"For the next few weeks and months, everything in your life is going to be about him and his welfare. You're going to have to put his needs above your own for a while. Your well-being is important, don't get me wrong, and you'll have support as well. But these next few steps are critical to his recovery, and he has to be our primary focus."

"Doc, since the day I met him, my life's been about him. That ain't gonna change any time soon."

Doctor Chang smiled, and I was pretty sure she wanted to say something like "You have no idea what you're in for" or "Naïve looks good on you." But the truth was, there wasn't anything I wouldn't do for him. I was all too aware just how much everything changed the day of his accident and how it would all change again once we told Justin some truths.

But we couldn't move forward if we weren't brave enough to take that first step.

"Are you ready?" she asked.

I nodded. "Yes."

"JUSTIN, can you tell me where you are?"

"Hospital," he answered after a second, and his words were slow.

Doctor Chang sat on one side of his bed; I sat on the other. We'd explained we were going to be asking questions. The truth was, the doc would be asking. I would just be sitting in. She wanted me to be a part of his recovery, but I was to remain impartial. I had to answer directly, without personal input.

"Do you know why you're in hospital?" Doctor Chang asked.

He paused and concentrated. "Car accident?"

"Do you remember the accident?"

"No." He shook his head. "Someone told me."

"Who told you that?"

He frowned. "Don't know."

"You were in an accident. The van you were driving was hit by a truck," she said plainly. "You took a hard hit to your head, and you're having trouble remembering things."

He gave a small nod. "My head hurts."

"Do you know which city the hospital is in?"

"Darwin."

My heart squeezed, but Doctor Chang continued like that was an expected answer. "Justin, you're in Newcastle, New South Wales."

He squinted as though he was trying to join invisible dots. "I don't live in Newcastle anymore. Moved away."

"You moved to Darwin when you were twenty-three, and you spent two years there. Then you moved back to Newcastle."

"Why?"

"You grew up in Newcastle. Do you remember that?"

He gave another small nod, though somewhat delayed. "Yeah. I went to school there. Got my apprenticeship. I worked at, uh . . ." He swallowed hard. "Newtown Road . . ." He squinted as though he couldn't quite grasp the details.

"Do you know how old you are?"

He stared at her for a long moment. "Um, twenty-five."

My heart gave another painful squeeze.

The doc put the motorbike magazine in front of him and he smiled at the cover. It was a photo of a KTM dirt bike and its rider sliding in mud. But then the doc put her finger in the top corner. "Can you read this fine print here?"

The truth was, we weren't sure about the cognitive damage done to skills like reading and writing, if he could read at all, or what the words would mean to him if he could.

He leaned forward a tiny bit, squinting at the issue date of the magazine. It was the newest one, the most current. It took some time to process, but we knew the moment he had. He shot a look to Doctor Chang, then to me. He could read it, all right. And the confusion in his eyes told me he understood.

"Justin, you turned thirty this year."

He shook his head. "No, didn't."

The doc showed him a photo on my phone. "Do you recognise this person?"

It was taken at his thirtieth birthday party, and the photo was of him with his arm around his sister. He blinked. "'S Becca."

Oh, thank God. He remembered her, at least.

"That's right," Doctor Chang said. "And this was your thirtieth birthday."

He swallowed hard and looked away from the photo. The doc handed me my phone with a nod. She was about to get to the hard part.

"Justin, do you remember anything about the people you might have dated?"

His eyes flashed to her then, full of fire and caution. "I uh . . . no . . . I'm not seeing anyone."

Again, my heart burned.

"Do you remember any of the men or women you might have dated?"

There it was. The word *men*.

His jaw bulged and he closed his eyes. His sexuality had been such an issue for him when he was younger, and I could only assume he remembered *that* all too well. It wasn't until he met me that he really accepted being his true self.

"You have a troubled relationship with your mother because she never approved of you being gay. Is that right, Justin?" Doctor Chang pushed gently.

He flinched, even with his eyes closed. After a deep breath, he opened his eyes but didn't look at us. "She doesn't . . . she never . . ."

"There's absolutely nothing wrong with being gay," she whispered, touching his hand. "You're safe here, and you've got some amazing friends here in Newcastle who love you just the way you are."

His gaze shot to hers. Then he looked away and licked his lips. "Don't remember . . ."

"Do you remember Dallas?" she asked, gesturing to me.

Justin glanced at me, then back to her. "He was here before. He works here, I think. I don't know . . ."

God, the ache . . .

"He doesn't work here. He's here to see you, Justin."

Justin swallowed hard but didn't say anything, and I didn't dare breathe.

"Justin, you live with Dallas. You live with him, and you work together. You're both motorbike mechanics at his shop in Wallsend, Newcastle."

He looked to me then, startled, disbelieving. I felt like I could vomit.

"Dallas is your boyfriend, Justin. You've been together for four and a half years. You live together."

He shook his head. "No."

Doctor Chang took my phone again and showed him the photos we'd agreed on. Me and him laughing, me and him holding hands, cuddling on the couch, kissing . . .

His expression didn't change. If anything, the only noticeable difference was the tiredness that seemed to settle over him. His blinks became suddenly slower, as though his eyelids had quickly become too heavy to keep open. He licked his lips but seemed to have difficulty in swallowing. "Don't remember . . ." He frowned and a tear escaped the corner of his eye. "Don't remember any of . . . what you're telling me . . . I can't . . ."

"It's a lot of information to process," Doctor Chang said gently. "I can see you're tired."

He closed his eyes, his face a bruised and swollen mask of sadness.

"I'll be back again tomorrow and we can talk some more."

He didn't reply. He was already asleep.

Doctor Chang turned and gave me a small smile. "That's step one."

Only a million to go.

"Tomorrow we'll see if he's retained anything we've discussed today."

Christ.

I tried to nod, to speak, to acknowledge her somehow, but I was too busy trying not to cry.

JUSTIN WAS STILL ASLEEP when I left at the end of morning visiting hours, and I had absolutely no idea what to expect when I returned.

Would he even want to see me? Would he ask me to leave? Would he ask me a hundred questions?

Would he remember the conversation at all?

One good thing that came from Justin's session with Doctor Chang, was that he knew he was gay. He'd had a real rough time in his teen years, and he'd struggled a lot. His mother rejected him when he was eighteen, and he'd fought hard to be true to himself.

It was hard enough for him to endure that once. The thought of him having to relive that a second time was torture.

So if there was one good thing I could take away from this morning's session, it was that at least Justin knew that about himself. There was so much of his life missing, but that fundamental truth was still there.

He was awake when I got there after his rest time was over. He was propped up in bed, and the blankets were pulled back off his right leg so I could see it properly for the first time. It wasn't bandaged fully. The scars would need to heal first. There was a reddish-purple line of staples on the outside of his thigh and one down his shin.

It looked painful.

He saw me and pulled his table closer, like it was a

shield. But then stopped himself and he swallowed hard, then winced.

I tried to smile for him but was sure I didn't quite pull it off. "Hey. Is it okay if I come in?"

He stared at me for a long, heart-stopping moment, and I was certain he was about to say no, but he gave a small nod. "I um . . . I can't remember your name . . ."

There was that pain in my heart again. My eyes burned but I blinked it all away. "My name is Dallas. Dallas Muller."

"Dallas," he whispered, like he was trying the word for the first time. Maybe he was hoping it would ring some distant bell. It clearly didn't. He shook his head.

I noticed he hadn't eaten much of anything off his plate. The fact he was eating actual food was a good sign, but his sandwich sat untouched, and a plate of diced fruit salad looked like it'd been pecked at. "Food's no good, huh?"

He made a face. "Not hungry."

"That sandwich has tomato on it," I said, trying to sound cheerful. "I'm sure I could bring you something that you actually like, if you want."

He considered that for a drawn-out few seconds. "Do you know what I like?"

Shit. I had to phrase things so carefully. "Well, the doc probably wouldn't be too happy, but if I happened to bring in some KFC at dinner time and accidently leave it on your table, you might not mind."

He looked at me then and his lip quirked, and I thought for a heart-splitting second that he might actually smile. But no, he didn't. "I might not mind."

I put the bag I was carrying on the seat and pulled out some magazines. "I thought you might like to read through these." I slid the four latest dirt bike magazines onto his table, pushing his discarded food tray to the side. The truth was, he'd read these magazines a dozen times, but he wouldn't remember that. And at least with the dirt bike magazines, he could just look at the pictures if reading was too much of a strain.

He eyed them and gave a nod. "Uh, thanks."

"No problem."

He looked at the bag I'd brought with me for a bit and made a face, so I picked it up. "I brought myself an iced coffee on the way here," I explained, taking the brown plastic bottle out of the bag. They were our weekend treats when we got groceries. Full of caffeine and sugar, Justin loved them. I honestly hadn't brought it for him—he'd been so reluctant to eat anything, I didn't think he'd want anything with milk in it. But he looked twice at it, and his eyes shot to mine.

I had no idea if he remembered it, if it triggered anything, or if he just wanted it. But it was the first time I'd seen any kind of recognition since he woke up. "Iced coffee," I said, holding it out to him. "You want it?"

He stared at me in that slow-processing way he did now, then opened his mouth to say something before deciding not to.

I twisted the lid off the bottle and smiled at him. "I won't tell the nurses you had a sip if you don't." He wasn't supposed to be having caffeine but a tiny sip wouldn't hurt...

He gave the smallest of nods, so I gently put it to his mouth and he had a small sip. He tasted it for a long few seconds before he swallowed. But then he hummed and closed his eyes, and the left corner of his mouth ever so slowly lifted upward.

I could have just about burst with happiness. I wanted to weep from the force of it.

Such a small step. A tiny, tiny step. But, oh my God, it was worth it.

"I'll keep it here for you," I said quietly.

He opened his eyes. Well, his left one. His right one was still badly swollen, though it was looking better every day. "I like that," he murmured. "Iced coffee."

"Yes, you do."

He closed his eyes again, though he seemed peaceful. I wouldn't want to assume that he was happy I was there, but he was okay with me being in his room, and he hadn't asked me to leave, which I took as a good thing. So I sat in my usual seat, grabbed one of his magazines, turned to page one and started reading it aloud.

CHAPTER FIVE

ALMOST TWO WEEKS after his accident, his sister, Rebecca, arrived to see him. She'd caught the early train up from Sydney on the Saturday, and I met her at the entrance of the hospital, to save her trying to find her way through the wards. She looked bone-tired, like all single mums who worked two jobs, but she was relieved to see me. I greeted her with a kiss to the cheek.

"How is he?"

"He's okay. He's working with the different doctors every day, like the physio and the neuro specialists."

"He still can't remember?"

"No. He may never regain those years, but we're hopeful."

She stopped walking. "He doesn't remember you at all?"

I shook my head.

"Christ, Dallas. That's gotta be hard."

Hard, awful, excruciating, heartbreaking . . . "I'm just grateful he's alive."

She frowned. "Sorry I couldn't get away sooner."

"What do you mean, you couldn't juggle two jobs and two kids to hike a couple hundred kilometres at the drop of a hat?"

Her face softened, and she gave me a sad smile. "But still . . ."

"Like I said to you when it happened, he wasn't in any shape to see you anyway," I explained. "But he's getting better every day. He can see out of both eyes now."

"Oh God."

I brightened for her. "Come on. I told him I was going to find you. He was excited about you visiting, so we better not keep him waiting."

I took her bag for her, and together we walked to Justin's room. "Ugh, I hate hospitals," she mumbled as we got closer.

Yep, even after all these days, all the hours, I never got used to the smell. It was cloying and awful. The neuro ward was quieter than most, and darker. Most patients here had noise and light sensitivities, Justin included.

I stopped her at the door. "He doesn't do too good with loud noises or bright lights. His headaches are bad, and he has aphasia, which is trouble remembering some words. But if he asks questions, be honest. He knows he has amnesia but it's confusing, so if he mentions anything that doesn't quite gel, we need to gently steer him back on course."

"Okay," she whispered, then took an unsteady breath.

I nodded to his room. "He's waiting."

I'd explained his injuries to Rebecca before, but nothing quite prepared you for seeing your loved one in a hospital bed all bandaged and bruised.

The bed was slightly inclined so he was kind of sitting up. He had his injured leg out from under the blankets again, his lines of staples on full display. The matching scar on his head was bandaged, and I was thankful Rebecca didn't have to see that. But the right side of his face was now a horror show of black, purple, green, and yellow. His right eye was open. Though it was bloodshot, he thankfully still had vision.

He'd had tests on his vision and hearing, focusing on the right side, where the most damage was, and the docs were pleasantly surprised to find all circuitry was still intact. Though when the doc had shone a penlight in his right eye, Justin had puked on him as thanks. He said it felt like the light pierced his brain and the pain was unbearable. He'd shaken and moaned, curling in on himself, and it was a short, sharp reminder of his injuries.

But yeah, while I knew it was bad, I was so used to seeing him lying in bed all banged up that I'd forgotten the shock it was for others. Rebecca put her hand to her mouth and got all teary. "Holy shit," she cried.

Justin looked at her, then looked again. His smile was wide. "Becca?"

She went to him and hugged him carefully, and she fussed over him and he stared up at her like he couldn't believe what he was seeing . . .

And it occurred to me, like a jolt to the heart, what the difference was.

He remembered her.

He was, for the first time since he woke up, seeing someone he remembered, seeing someone he knew.

And it wasn't me.

I was no more than a stranger that he was polite to, like his nurses and doctors.

And all of a sudden, the room felt too small, too hot, and it was much too much. I put Becca's bag down by the chair. "I'll just let you catch up," I said to no one in particular. I didn't know if they heard me. I simply slipped out of the room and made my way back to the main entrance.

I needed air.

Just ten minutes. I just needed some fresh air in my lungs, to take some deep breaths and clear the swirls panicking in my mind. I knew he didn't remember me. I was very well aware. It shouldn't have come as such a surprise, but I guess seeing it with my own two eyes was different.

I stood outside and leaned against the wall. It was a little overcast; the air was cool and the sun was warm on my skin. I closed my eyes and concentrated on my breathing until I no longer felt like crying or screaming.

I need to get my shit together. I was in this for the long haul, for however long it took. Every nurse, every doctor had told me a thousand times there would be hurdles and setbacks, and some days would be nothing but backward steps.

But this wasn't a setback for Justin. This was a milestone for him. He finally remembered someone from his past, a face, a name, memories, recognition, dots that finally joined on their own. Justin finally got matching pieces of the puzzle that was his past.

I needed to recognise that and be happy for him. I needed to find Doctor Chang and tell her of this breakthrough. Because that's what this was. What did she tell me? All those days ago? That everything was about him, it needed to be about him. This wasn't about me. How could it be? I needed to remove my pain, square it away for another day, for a conversation with a therapist or someone . . .

I needed to be there for Justin, and I had a sense of urgency to get back to him. So I called past the cafeteria, using coffees as an excuse for my disappearance. I even bought a small decaf cappuccino for Justin. I added sugar and asked for it to be lukewarm so he didn't burn his mouth.

One thing I had noticed over the last week was how he no longer paused to think if something might be hot or cold. It was just food or drink, and he would simply put it in his mouth. Not that he ate a great deal, and not that hospital food was ever scalding hot, but cups of tea sometimes were. And he would quite often take a sip without giving it time to cool, which had made him reluctant to drink any tea or coffee at all.

I knocked on the door to announce my arrival, with a tray of takeout coffee cups in hand. Rebecca was sitting in my usual seat, holding his hand. The tears were gone, and Justin looked tired. His blinks were slow, but he looked happy.

"Anyone for coffee?"

"Oh, you're a doll," Bec said, taking hers. "Thank you so much."

I pulled Justin's table over and sat his coffee in front of him. "I got one for you too. It's not too hot, and I got them to add some sugar."

He blinked up at me and gave a slight nod, making no attempt to lift his left arm, so I held the cup to his lips and he took a small sip. "'S good."

"It's proper coffee," I said, giving him as big a smile as I could manage. He didn't need to know it was decaf. "How does your arm feel? Can you hold the cup?"

He'd been working on some weakness in his left arm with the physio. There was nothing broken or sprained with his left arm, but brain injuries did strange things to bodies, and sometimes he wouldn't even attempt to use it. His broken arm, apart from being broken, was understandable. But there was nothing actually wrong with his left arm, and the physio had told me to encourage him to use it, which was why I asked him.

He looked at his arm and raised it heavily onto the table. "Yeah," he said. "'S all right."

I held the cup for him while he grasped it and stood ready as he slowly lifted it to his mouth. He took a sip and put the cup back down all without incident, just a little slower than usual.

Bec watched on, then her gaze flickered to mine with a flash of sadness before she smiled back at her brother. "I was just telling Jussy that I spoke to our mother. Nothing's changed there." She gave me a pissed-off raised eyebrow before smiling back at Justin. "And then I was telling him about the girls."

Their mother had always been horrible, so I couldn't say I was surprised. But the girls were a much happier topic. "Oh," I said, giving her a meaningful look. "Have you got any recent photos of them on your phone? I'm sure he'd love to see them."

She clued in and quickly pulled out her phone. "Oh, sure." She showed him the screen. "This was Phoebe's costume for book week."

His eyes shot to hers. "No. She . . . That's not . . . she . . . walking . . ."

Bec looked to me for help. "Justin," I said gently. "Phoebe is six now."

He looked at me, then at Becca, then at the screen. "She is?"

"Yep," Bec said, teary again. "She had her birthday just two months ago. You sent her a *Frozen* backpack and lunchbox."

His eyes went wide. "I did?" God, he'd spent an hour trying to pick the right one . . .

Bec nodded. "And she loves it." She swiped to another photo. "And here's Holly playing soccer."

Justin looked at all the photos Bec showed him of the girls over the last few years. He shook his head in disbelief, and while he was clearly exhausted, there was a deeper understanding in the sadness.

Bec put her phone away and cupped his face. "You okay, Jussy? Do you need to sleep?"

He slow blinked, almost not opening his eyes again. "Tired."

"We'll let you get some sleep," she said, looking to me again.

I nodded. "It's almost rest time anyway. We'll be back at three. Just like always, soon as they open the doors, I'll be here."

"And Bec?" he asked, trying to open his eyes.

She put a hand on his arm. "I'll be back too."

He sagged then and succumbed to sleep. I fixed his bed so he was lying down flat, pulled up the blanket, and moved the table out of the way. Then I led Becca out, and neither of us spoke until we reached the cafeteria.

I ordered us some toasted sandwiches and more coffee, and when I sat opposite Bec, she shook her head. Tears threatened to spill but didn't. "He's um . . . He's . . ."

"He's doing much better," I offered.

"He really doesn't remember."

"No. But he remembered you, and that's a good thing. And the girls. He *remembered* them. He hasn't really remembered much since he woke up. He's been taking in what we tell him, but today it was like a light went on. And that's a real good thing." I sighed. "And honestly, I think seeing the photos of them was good for him. Hard, but good. We can tell him he's no longer in Darwin and we can say he's missing some years, but I don't think he ever really understood. He doesn't remember me at all, so I'm not a gauge of time for him. And you might have aged a little, but not that he would probably notice too much. But the girls . . . last he remembered, Phoebe was still in nappies and now she's in school. That's a big change."

Bec nodded and chewed on her bottom lip. "Do you think he'll get better?"

I sighed and turned the coffee cup in my hand. "I asked the brain doc that in the beginning, and she said better wasn't the right word. Will his body heal? Will his leg and arm mend? Yes. Will his brain? We don't know. Will Justin ever be who he was before the accident? No." I put the cup down and pushed the half-eaten sandwich away. "Brain injuries change a person forever. Even if he remembered everything tomorrow, he'd still have headaches and dizziness and issues with light and noise. Even if he comes good and is right as rain for years, ten years from now he might still have setbacks and bouts of headaches, or one day wake up with slurred speech. We just don't know. But we do know this is a long-term thing."

She got teary again. "Thank God he has you. This can't be easy for you, and I'm sorry I can't be more help."

"It's not easy," I admitted. "But I love him."

She reached over and squeezed my hand. "And he loves you. From the second he saw you, he did. You should have heard how excited he was when he first told me about you. He was head over heels in love from day one. He will remember that. I know he will."

Now it was me who got teary. "I hope so. If not, he'll just have to fall in love with me all over again." I tried to smile, to laugh it off, but couldn't manage it. Because what if he didn't? "And if he doesn't . . . Well, I'll do whatever he needs to be happy. Because that's what you do when you love someone, right? You'd do anything to make them happy. Even if that means letting them go."

A tear ran down Becca's cheek and she wiped it away. "It wasn't just *his* world that got turned upside down by a truck that day, was it?"

I shook my head but couldn't answer until I was sure my voice would hold. "No. Not just me, either. The boys at the shop are covering for the both of us. Davo's basically running the whole place. I'd be lost without them. Justin doesn't remember them at all either."

She took a deep breath. "Is there something we can do to help him remember?"

"We can't plant any of our memories in his head. We can just show him things and hope he remembers on his own."

"Like the photos of the girls."

"Exactly."

"Have you shown him photos of you and him together?"

"Some, just on my phone. A few days ago," I replied. "I was going to get some printed. They have a kiosk thing, but I couldn't figure it out and I ran out of time."

She brightened. "Where's the kiosk?"

"Just down the road. Why? Do you know how to use them?"

She smiled, grabbing her bag. "Sure I do. We'll print them off, then he can look at them all day long. He will remember you, Dallas. I know he will."

WE GOT BACK RIGHT on three o'clock when the doors opened for visiting hours again. Matt, the nurse, gave me a smile. I was familiar with most of the staff on the neuro ward now, and they knew me. "Brought him lunch again," he said warmly, nodding to the bag I was holding. Then he gave me a wink. "Can't say I blame him for not wanting hospital food."

"Is he awake?" I asked.

"He was about ten minutes ago. Physio's been in. Wants him up on his feet tomorrow."

"That's a good thing, right?"

Matt smiled. "I'd reckon so."

Justin was awake when we got there. He was frowning at the menu in front of him on the table. "Hey," I said softly as we walked in.

He looked up and gave me a small smile, but then he saw Bec behind me and he gave her a real smile. I pretended it didn't burn all the way through and put the bag on his bed near his leg. "I brought you a juice and a water," I said, putting them on the table. They were the pop-top kind so he didn't have to worry about unscrewing lids, and I'd already removed the seals. "And one of these."

It was a lunch snack box that was full of things he could pick at: grapes, salted pretzels, cheese cubes, and some crackers with a small tub of hummus. I'd bought him one before, and it was the most he'd eaten in a while.

He inspected everything I put in front of him, then he looked at me. "Thanks," he said politely before searching for his sister.

I stood back and let Bec in closer. "Whatcha got here?" she asked, sliding the menu closer. "Do you need to fill this out?"

"Think so." He stared at the sheet of paper and frowned. "Don't know what I like. And I read the . . . but I can't remember . . . And I can't hold the pen too good with

53

this hand." He lifted his left hand and let it fall back beside him.

"Would you like Dallas to fill it in for you?" Bec asked.

I went to the right side of his bed and turned the menu around to face me. "It's a bit hard to write with your left when you're right-handed," I said casually. "What about some toast and tea for breakfast, and I'll bring you in an iced coffee when I get here?" They had decaf ones and it wasn't like he'd know the difference . . .

He gave a nod.

"And for lunch, if I order the sandwich but I bring you something, then you can choose which you feel like the most."

He nodded again. "I like this," he said, slowly reaching for the snack box I bought him.

"Then I'll bring you one every day," I said, making a mental note to call into the supermarket on the way home. It'd be cheaper if I made it myself and brought it with me. Now that he was actually eating food . . . "And for dinner," I continued. "They have fish or cottage pie, so I'll put the cottage pie." I was going to add "because you don't really like fish" but stopped myself.

Justin picked at his grapes and pretzels and cheese, then reached for his water. I was tempted to get it for him, to help him drink it, but thought it must have been bad enough not being able to tick boxes on a menu. The least I could let him do was take a drink by himself. As long as he was comfortable moving his left arm, I was comfortable in letting him.

"So, Jussy," Bec began. "I wanted to show you some more photos. You think you're up for that?"

"Hmm," he agreed as he sipped his water. Then he ate

another grape. Food he could hold in one hand and pick at was definitely the way to go.

Bec and I had agreed that the photos would be best coming from her. He remembered her, he knew her, he trusted her. She stood up by his arm and held out the first photo. We'd mixed a few, from her phone and mine, so there'd be some faces he recognised. "Here's you and me at your birthday dinner last year," she said. "You and Dallas came down to Sydney and stayed with me and the girls for the weekend."

"And here's you with both Phoebe and Holly," she said, showing the next photo. The girls were in their pyjamas, tackling him on the couch, the three of them laughing.

He squinted. "That's really them," he murmured, shaking his head like he couldn't believe it. Not that he didn't believe her, just that he didn't believe he was missing so much time.

Bec nodded. "And here's one of Dallas and the girls." In this photo, Phoebe had her arms around my neck, and I was holding a laughing Holly under my arm like a football. We thought it might be good for Justin to see that I was part of his missing pieces. His nieces knew me, they loved me. They called me Uncle Dallas . . .

"And here's you at work," she said, moving to the next photo. It was a picture of him sitting on a client's brand new KTM dirt bike. They'd called into the shop to show it off, and Justin just had to sit on it and take it for a bit of a ride through the shop and out into the car park. His grin was almost from ear to ear.

His eyes shot to Bec. "That mine?"

"No," I answered for her. "It was a client's bike. He brought it in to show you. Your bike is a bit older than that."

He looked up at me. "Have a bike?"

"You do, yes. A 2016 KTM 450 SX-F. There's a photo in there."

His smile widened. "KTM?"

"You wouldn't own anything else." The truth was, he'd always wanted one. It was his dream bike, and for his thirtieth birthday, I bought him a new second-hand one.

But more on the photos . . . I pointed to a guy in the background of the photo he was holding. "That's Davo. He came in to see you last week."

Justin frowned and shook his head. He didn't remember him.

The next photo made my heart thump against my ribs. It was a selfie, of me and him, our arms around each other. I was smiling at the camera but he was smiling at me. "Here's you and Dallas. Goofing off on the couch by the look of it," Bec said fondly.

We'd just got home from the footy and it was freezing. I was set to cook dinner, but he wanted pizza and he'd pulled me onto the couch, tickled me, and kissed me until I gave in. It was one of my favourite photos, and the memory of how that night had ended in bed . . .

Justin stared at the photo, like really stared at it. "I don't . . . Don't remember . . ." Then he looked up to me. "Sorry."

"That's okay," I replied when it was obviously very, very not okay. "It's not your fault."

Bec moved on to the next photo. "Here's you at the beach. Two years ago?" she asked me.

I nodded. "Yep. We went up to Halliday Point for the weekend."

He frowned again, and I wondered if it was too much. The doc said it was okay— good, even— to show him photos, but that frown and the line between his eyebrows kind of told me he'd had enough.

"Wish I could 'member," he mumbled, closing his eyes.

Bec gave me a sad smile and put the photos on his table. "It's okay, Jussy."

"No 's not," he replied. When he opened his eyes, they were teary. "Missing so much. I wish could . . . but it's just not there. It feels like I'm . . . like it's all some . . . joke. Except for my arm and my leg and m'fucking head hurts. God."

I wanted to touch him, to pull him into my arms and hold him and tell him everything would be okay. I wanted to kiss the side of his head and rub his back while he slept . . .

But I couldn't even hold his hand.

I had to clamp my mouth shut and my hands were fists at my side. "It'll get easier," I whispered.

He wouldn't look at me, and that probably hurt more than anything.

Bec took his left hand. "Jussy, I know it's hard right now. It's okay to be scared. And to be pissed off that everything you know was taken away from you. But you gotta know how much you are loved. Me and the girls, we love you. And Dallas loves you so much."

Justin screwed his face up, then winced, and tears escaped.

And I still couldn't touch him, I couldn't fill in the blanks for him. But I could tell him the truth. "I do love you, Justin," I said, ignoring the burn in my eyes and the lump in my throat. "I know that must seem strange to you right now. But I won't give up on you. You're not alone in this. I'll be with you, however you need me. I don't expect anything from you. I just want you to be happy and healthy. That's all."

His face twisted as if in pain, and another tear escaped. "So tired," he said with a groan. "Hurts."

Bec put a hand on his arm and kissed his temple. "Go to sleep. I gotta get going if I'm gonna catch my train. But I'll call you tomorrow."

He opened his eyes slowly, exhausted. "'Kay."

"Love you, Justin," she said.

He almost nodded but fell asleep.

Bec wiped her tears away, and when she looked at me, she had that fierceness that was obviously a family trait. I'd seen it in Justin's eyes a thousand times.

"He will remember you," she said, her bottom lip trembling. "He will remember how much you love him. I know he will."

CHAPTER SIX

DOCTOR ANDERSON FINISHED ASKING Justin his usual round of questions, then took one look at me and frowned. "You need to look after yourself too," he said. "Not sleeping?"

I shook my head but plastered on a fake smile in front of Justin. "I'm fine."

He sighed, because this was obviously a conversation he had with the loved ones of his patients all the time, but his expression was kind. "Do I need to remind you that you can't look after him if you don't look after yourself?"

"No, I got that, thanks."

He clapped me on the shoulder just as two other doctors arrived. "Okay, Justin," the physio said. "We're gonna get you up and on your feet today." Justin had been doing exercises from his bed, leg bending, that kind of thing. But they needed to wait because of his head. Vertigo and a fall or severe headaches and nausea were serious issues with brain injuries. But they reckoned he was ready, so . . .

Justin glanced to me, then swallowed hard. "I don't know."

The physio was undeterred. He explained what he was going to do in a no-nonsense voice that gave no room for argument; how he would stand on his left foot for three seconds and they would hold his weight. First they sat him up and let his head catch up with the movement; then they gently lowered his feet to the floor and let him sit like that for a few minutes.

He was already pale, but he kept searching for me, which made me happier than it should've. I gave him an encouraging nod each time. Because if he could do this, we were one step closer to going home.

One small step.

"Okay, Justin, on three."

"One."

He looked up at me, scared but determined.

"Two."

He took a deep breath.

"Three."

They lifted him and he stood on his left foot for one second, two seconds, but then his head fell forward and I shot to him as if to catch him. But he was well supported, and they put him back on the bed. He was white as a sheet now, sweat beaded on his brow, and he was breathing heavy.

"You did great, Justin," the doc said. The neuro and the physio both fussed over him for a bit and left the nurses to get him comfortable again. I thought he might vomit, but he didn't.

Soon enough it was just me and him. He had his eyes closed, though he had a bit more colour. A tear ran down to his temple. "You did real good," I whispered.

"Head hurts," he breathed.

He looked so helpless, so fragile, that I couldn't help

myself. I had to comfort him somehow and let him know he wasn't alone. I took his hand in both of mine. "You're okay, Justin. You're not alone. Everything will be okay."

Another tear escaped, but he squeezed my fingers and never let go until sleep relaxed his grip.

SOMETHING HAD CHANGED for Justin when he woke up. He was different toward me. The polite smiles once afforded to a stranger were now something else. I didn't want to overthink it, but the look he gave me was something closer to how he'd look at a friend.

And that was a pretty big fucking deal.

I must have dozed off in the seat beside him, listening to his peaceful breathing, only to be woken up by a machine beeping. I jolted upright to find a nurse at one of his machines, changing something. "Didn't mean to wake you," she said apologetically.

And Justin smiled at me. "Was wondering if you'd wake up."

I rubbed the crick in my neck. "I didn't mean to fall asleep, sorry."

But he was still smiling. Not quite like he'd smiled at his sister, but different to how he smiled at the nurses and doctors.

I didn't want to question it. I didn't want him to stop it or second guess himself. I'd take anything he could give me, and if that was a slight quirk of his lips, I'd gladly take it.

I checked my phone for the time just as his lunch tray was delivered, but he took one look at the plate of mixed sandwiches and frowned. "Here, I'll swap you," I said, taking his sandwiches and producing the packed lunch I'd made for him. It was similar to the ones I'd bought for him—a container split into sections for different snacks—but I added a few things I knew he liked. Well, things he used to like. Like some of those soy crisps and the sweet and salty popcorn, along with some grapes and cubed cheese, and I even threw in a few M&M's. Things he could pick at with one hand, that didn't require a great deal of chewing, and things that didn't crunch too loud in his head.

I took the sandwich and began to eat it, and he did the same, using his left hand slowly, but using it nonetheless.

"The doc said you're not sleeping," he said between mouthfuls. It wasn't posed as a question, but it kind of was.

I finished chewing and swallowed. "Uh, yeah."

He was quiet for a while, lifting some popcorn to his mouth and chewing methodically. "Because of me."

Jesus.

I certainly couldn't say it was because I hated sleeping alone and how I missed him most at night. How I missed the way he searched for me, even in his sleep, and how he'd wrap himself around me like a freaking koala every night. It used to annoy me sometimes, and now I missed it so much it hurt. "I'm just worried, that's all."

He frowned as he ate a grape, and I gave him all the time he needed to process what was said, and perhaps what he was trying to say. "Sorry I don't remember you," he said.

I tried to smile for him but gave up. "It's not your fault."

"Wish I did," he said, so quietly I wasn't sure he meant to say it out loud. When I met his gaze, he was looking right at me. "You're here a lot, and Becca liked you, so you gotta be all right."

My heart felt like it could burst, and I almost cried. Instead, it all came out as a laugh. "Yeah, I'm all right."

"You're not exactly . . ." He squinted at me. "I can't

think of the word." He shut his eyes. "Why can't I think of some words?"

You're not exactly . . . *I'm not exactly what? Jesus, don't leave me hanging on that.*

"It's the aphasia," I said gently. "It means you have trouble with some words some of the time. It's random."

He sighed and opened his eyes slowly, suddenly looking tired. "It's like my brain is bogged, ya know? Like the wheels are spinning but the back wheel can't . . . hold." Pretty sure *hold* wasn't the word he wanted, but I didn't correct him. His right eye closed and I wondered if his headache was getting worse. "Like the things I want to see are all misty."

That was the most he'd said to me, the most honest he'd been with me since his accident. I smiled at him, a proper smile, no faking or trying. An actual fucking smile. "That makes sense. And it's still early days yet. The mist might clear and you'll be able to see."

He looked from me to the snack box. "And if it doesn't?"

"Then we find new ways. We work on different things."

"We . . . ," he said softly.

Oh hell. What if he didn't want that? What if he didn't want me to be a part of his life anymore?

I opened my mouth to say something—say what, I had no clue—just as a nurse came in. "Visiting time is up. You'll have to come back after three."

I nodded woodenly, sure if I moved too fast, I'd splinter into a thousand pieces.

What if he didn't want there to be a *we* or an *us*? What if his life, after this, didn't include me?

"Hey, can I ask you something?" Justin said to the nurse.

"Sure," she replied, walking in closer.

63

"What's the word . . . I can't think of the word for pretty but not. Opposite of that."

"The opposite of pretty?" she clarified, eyeing me cautiously.

"Yeah. There's a word. Not ugly. That's not the word . . . Jesus, why can't I think of the word."

"Unattractive?" she hedged, clearly not sure where he was going with this. I had no clue either.

"Yes. That's it," Justin said excitedly, but I could see he was tired. "I wanted to say he wasn't unattractive. That's the word."

"What?" I asked, confused.

"You," he said, a lazy smile on his lips. "I said you weren't exactly unattractive."

Oh.

Oh.

"Oh!" I barked out a laugh. "Right. Um, thanks?"

The nurse laughed, probably relieved, but tapped her wrist in a time's-up fashion as she walked out.

I could not believe he said that to me! I had absolutely no chance of trying to hide how happy that made me. "You're not exactly unattractive either, you know," I said. "I'll be back after three."

I left him then, feeling on cloud nine. It wasn't that he thought I was good looking, that even with no memory of me whatsoever he still thought I was good looking. It was that he smiled at me like he was comfortable with me, that I wasn't a stranger. And how he spoke to me about how he was feeling and what it felt like to not be able to remember things . . .

I was still smiling when I got back to the shop. Davo looked at me and then did a double-take. "Holy shit, is he . . . ? Did he remember something?"

"Nah, not really," I said. "It was just a good morning. It was small." I held up my fingers, barely a centimetre apart. "But I saw a glimpse of him today. Justin's still in there."

"For real?"

"He said something funny, and he kinda said he thought I was good looking."

Davo's grin widened. "Yep. That sounds like him all right."

I laughed, and so help me God, it felt good to actually laugh. "I mean, it could all be different when I go back, and he might be having a real shit afternoon and not want me in his room when I get there, but this morning was good. And I'll take all the small steps forward I can get."

"Speaking of a real shit afternoon," he said, still grinning. "That pile of mail on your desk isn't getting any smaller."

I gave a nod, and after neglecting my business for two weeks, went into my office.

JUSTIN WASN'T in a shit mood when I went back. He was just tired. Physio really took it out of him, but he never really complained. The docs had said that we could expect outbursts of anger and misdirected rage, as was common with brain injuries, but I had yet to see that in him.

He wasn't the type to get angry before his accident. Actually, he hated aggression and confrontation, so maybe I shouldn't have been surprised that there were no bouts of temper. Not to say there wouldn't ever be . . . I knew all too well that frustration made people lash out, but Justin was more inclined to retreat into himself. He wouldn't sulk, but he went quiet, trying to figure stuff out in his head—and now, well, his mind wouldn't cooperate.

"You okay?" I asked.

"Dunno," he mumbled. "Tired."

"Physio sucks, huh?"

He almost smiled. Almost. "Yeah. Doc said m' arm's getting better. And I'll be up on my feet again. Every day now."

"Oh, that's good, right?"

He made a face. "Was talking about going home."

Oh . . . Going home. There I was excited by the prospect, and he didn't even know if he had a home.

His gaze shot to mine before going back to his leg. "Yeah."

I pulled the seat closer to his bed so he could see me without having to turn his head. "Hey. You have a home."

"Do I?" He shot me a look. "'Cause I don't remember it. The last I remember was a shitty unit in Darwin, but that's not right anymore, is it?"

"No, it's not. You have a home here, in Newcastle. It's above the workshop, the mechanic shop. You have a place to go home to, where all your stuff is. And Squish."

He glanced at me then. "Squish?"

"Our cat."

He frowned. "*Our* cat . . . ?"

Fuck. "Sorry. *The* cat." My frown matched his.

"Sorry."

"Don't apologise." It wasn't his fault he didn't remember anything. He shouldn't have to apologise.

He let his head fall back on the pillow and closed his eyes with a long sigh. "I don't like being here," he whispered. "But at least it's . . ." He screwed up his face, trying to search for the right word but settled on a bit of a shrug when the word wouldn't come. "I know here. I don't know anywhere else but here."

I couldn't even tell him it would still be nice, though, to be surrounded by his own things because he didn't remember any of it. "Did the doc say when you might be leaving?"

"Week or so, maybe," he replied. His eyes were barely open and he was mumbling. "Said because of you. Look after me. Help recovery quick."

I covered his hand with mine. "Go to sleep, Juss. I'll be here when you wake up."

He took a deep breath in and was already asleep before he exhaled.

Going home . . . He was almost ready to go home. Was that too soon? For him?

For me?

What if I wasn't good at being someone's carer? What if he took a fall because I'd done something stupid like left the bathmat on the floor? What if he couldn't cope with the stairs?

What if he didn't want to live with me?

Certain Justin would be asleep for a while, I left him and went in search of his nurse, who pointed me in the direction of one of his doctors. She was just finishing up with another patient, and she smiled when she saw me.

"You look worried," Doctor Chang said, meeting me in the corridor. I knew she wasn't the expert on this in particular, but she'd spent so much time with us over the last week or so . . .

"Justin mentioned going home? How do I get ready for that? What if I suck at it?"

She smiled warmly. "I need a cup of tea. Come sit with me."

I followed her to the small break room and waited as she filled two cups with hot water, threw a teabag in each, and handed me one. Apparently I was drinking black tea now.

She sat in one of the chairs and waited for me to sit next to her. "Okay, first things first. Justin's doing well. All things considered, it could have been so much worse."

I know that. Jesus, I know that.

"His recovery is going well, and yes, we can think about him going home soon. Another week or even a couple of weeks." She sipped her tea. "But there are many things we need to do before then. Occupational therapist first. They will go to your house and suggest changes to make life easier for him."

I let out a relieved breath. "Okay, good. We have stairs."

She made a face. "Also, Justin needs to prove he can walk assisted, with crutches or some kind of mobility aide. Crutches might be difficult until his broken arm is healed. So yes, home is on the table, but he has some hard work to do yet." She looked me right in the eye. "He will have a lot of ongoing medical appointments and will need full-time care in the beginning. Help with bathing, using the toilet. It's not easy. And a home nurse will visit daily for a little while, but the bulk of responsibility will fall on you."

"Okay." I nodded. "That's fine."

She smiled and sipped her tea again. "The photos were a good idea. He was looking at them when I arrived today."

"He was?"

"Yep. He was looking at the photos of you both, but you in particular."

That made my heart do crazy things. "Oh."

She smiled at me. "He said you must be a kind person because you visit every day and you bring him iced coffee and food that he likes."

God, her words almost made me cry. "He said that?"

"And that you looked really worried after he tried to stand up for the first time, and that you held his hand when he cried."

I barked out a laugh and had to wipe my nose with the back of my hand. "I can't believe he said that." I took a shaky breath and shook away the tears. "I worried he wouldn't want anything to do with me when he woke up. Or even any day I walk into his room. I mean, he could say thanks but no thanks, couldn't he? He's not just missing memories of me, but he has no emotional attachment to me either. And that scares the hell out of me."

She stood up and stretched her shoulders. "He's trying to get the pieces to fit. Not the old pieces," she said. "But the new pieces in this new, confusing puzzle. He's trying, and that's a real good sign. There are no guarantees, of course. But he *is* trying."

She left me alone with a promise to see me again tomorrow, and with a heavy sigh, I took the awful cup of tea back into his room and waited for him to wake up.

THE DAYS that followed were much the same. Physio, both lying down and standing on his left leg and getting used to being upright. His head still got the better of him and he was dizzy and nauseous, and he was still tired as hell. But he was improving. He was almost using his left arm all the time, and his aphasia and slurred speech were only more pronounced when he was tired.

He had more CAT scans, more MRIs, and they modified his pain meds, and he had to take an entire pharmacy of pills every day.

But he *was* improving.

He smiled when I got there every morning. Which might have been only for the iced coffee I brought with me, but it was a smile nonetheless. He was eating more and his bones and scars were healing well, and by all accounts, his army of doctors was happy with his progress.

When I arrived with his iced coffee in hand, his bed was rumpled and empty. The bike magazines and photographs were spread all over his table; he'd obviously been looking at the photos again. He looked at them quite often, sometimes flipping through them like a deck of cards, sometimes studying each one.

A nurse I didn't know came in and began stripping his bed. "Uh, excuse me, but where is Justin?"

I mean, his things were still here, but he wasn't, and he'd never not been in here before . . .

"He not have a good night," she said in broken English. "They take him."

I turned her words over in my head. "Take him? Take him where?" *Don't panic, Dallas. It's probably nothing.* I tried to make my voice as calm as possible. "I'm sorry. Where did they take him?"

"Oh, hi, Dallas," Donna said. She was another nurse that I'd become quite familiar with. She looked after Justin a lot. "They've just taken him for a shower."

I almost buckled with relief. "Christ, why didn't she lead with that?"

Donna chuckled and helped remake the bed. They were like a pit-crew, taking efficient to a whole new level. Donna straightened the room up as the other nurse took the dirty linen to a huge hamper at the door. "He won't be long, I'm sure."

"Did he not have a good night? The other nurse said . . ."

"Apparently not."

"Was it pain? Did he try and get up by himself?"

She shook her head. "Nightmares," she whispered. "And if the nightmares aren't bad enough, he jolted awake and strained his arm."

"His right arm? The one he broke?"

She gave a nod. "He was okay, but a shower will help freshen him up. I'd imagine he'll be happy to see you."

"Yeah," I said, not feeling her confidence.

She gave me a sly smile. "He watches the door for you, you know."

"He does?" *Was I smiling? Or was my face as stunned as I was?*

She finished tidying with an amused smile. "He won't be long."

I slumped in the chair, trying to get my head around everything I'd just learned. If they were showering him, his arm must be okay. But the nightmares . . . that was new. Well, it was new to me.

Did he dream of the accident? Because he had no memory of that. But I could only imagine the scream of tires, twisted metal, and shattered glass. I'd seen photographs of the van and how they'd had to cut him out . . . Was that what he remembered?

I shuddered at the thought.

Movement at the door pulled me to my feet. Justin came through in a wheelchair, his right leg propped up out front. An orderly was pushing him, and his doctor followed him in.

"Hey," I said, taking in the sight of him. He looked all shower-fresh, and he was clean-shaven. He was obviously tired, but he smiled when he saw me. That familiar smile... "There you are."

The orderly and I helped him onto the bed, and I fixed his pillow for him and pulled the blanket up. It took him a second to catch his breath. "Hey," he murmured back.

The doctor propped Justin's pillow and Justin gave a nod. "Okay. No physio today, as long as you promise to keep using your left arm and move your left leg a bit for me, okay?"

Justin nodded slowly. "'Kay."

The doctor then looked at me. "Lots of rest today. I'd even go so far as to say maybe cut the visit short this morning and just come back this afternoon."

I opened my mouth to speak, but Justin spoke first. "He stay." He closed his eyes. "He can stay. Please."

Oh my God.

"I'll stay," I whispered, running my hand down his arm and taking his hand. "I'll stay right here."

His fingers squeezed my hand a little and his breathing evened out. He was already asleep.

The doctor sighed. "Make sure he rests."

"I will," I promised. "Doc? Did he say what the night-mares were about?"

The doctor looked to Justin, who was very much asleep, then back to me and shook his head. "He doesn't know exactly. Just darkness and fear."

My heavy heart sank to my feet.

"It's not uncommon," the doc said. "It wasn't the first time, and I can assume it won't be the last."

I nodded, and the warden scooted my chair over so I didn't have to let go of Justin's hand before they left me alone with him. "It's okay, baby," I whispered. "Whatever comes at us."

He didn't stir, not even a little bit, for most of the morning. I held his hand and studied his beautiful face. His bruises were mostly gone now, the cut above his eye had healed nicely. The hair where they'd shaved his head was growing back, hiding the L-shaped scar.

His dark hair, sun-kissed skin, his long eyelashes, his gently parted lips . . . He really was beautiful. And I hated that his independence had been taken away from him. I hated that his life had been turned inside out because of the truck, because of the rain, because of someone else. I hated that he was scared, and I hated that I couldn't fix everything and give him back what had been taken away.

It wasn't fair on him. He did nothing to deserve this shitty blow. And, selfishly, I hated that this had happened to me, to us. We'd had the perfect life, and in the blink of an eye, it was gone.

Deleted.

For Justin, it was as though it had never happened. The life we'd had, the love, me, us . . . completely erased.

The actions of someone else had taken it all away. I wanted to be mad, to find the truck driver and show him the damage he'd done, but I didn't have it in me. I just wanted Justin to be safe and loved. That was where my energy and focus had to be.

Sometime later, I was reading one of his bike magazines aloud to him when I felt eyes on me. ". . . The subframe is longer, and the swingarm has a longer adjustment slot. The most obvious change is that the bodywork is different . . ."

I glanced up from the page to see Justin smiling sleepily at me. "Keep going," he mumbled.

"I'm only reading the KTM articles, just so you know. Don't want you getting mad at me for filling your head full of Yamaha specs."

The corner of his mouth quirked upward, and I continued to read aloud to him, my voice deliberately soothing and melodic. Eventually his eyes opened and stayed open, and he watched me as I read through more of the magazine.

It warmed my heart, and I could only hope it did the same to him.

Eventually he tried to sit up a little, so I fixed his bed for him to be more upright. "Oh, I almost forgot," I said, handing him the iced coffee. "It's not super cold, but it'll be fine."

He sighed after the first sip. "Thank you."

"Had a rough night, huh?"

He grunted some kind of response, then said, "My brain is misty today."

He'd said before that his mind was misty, and I wondered if he meant foggy. It didn't matter. The message was clear. "The doc said you'd need rest today."

He slow blinked and gave a nod, and it was like we'd gone back two weeks in his recovery. They'd said his recovery would feel like two steps forward, one step back, and we'd had so many steps forward that this stumble felt huge.

I rubbed my chin and smiled for him. "You shaved. Looks good."

He almost smiled again. "Didn't. The guy did."

The nursing staff did it . . . "Well, he did a good job."

He slowly reached his left hand up to his face, then let his hand drop back down. He took another slow sip of his drink, then his eyes closed. "Read more? Like your voice . . ."

He liked my voice . . .

So I chose a different magazine and started at the beginning, pretending he couldn't hear the tears and hope in my words.

HE WAS BETTER the next day, almost like he hadn't had a bad day the day before. And two days later, his recovery seemed to be back on track.

He'd obviously had a better night's sleep, and his morning physio wasn't horrible. He was bending his leg okay and lifting his bandaged arm, and he was able to stand for a bit. He even put the foot of his injured leg on the floor.

"I liked the chair," he told Doctor Chang. "With the . . ." He scowled. He pointed to the door. "With the . . ."

"The wheelchair?" she asked.

"Yeah. Wheelchair."

"You liked being out of this room, being mobile and seeing other people, and getting out of this room?" she asked. "Did I mention getting out of this room?"

Justin's smile almost became a grin. "Yes."

She was serious then. "Do you think you're up for it?"

"Dunno. I want to try." He swallowed hard. "Can I try?"

She gave him a fond smile. "I think so. When do you think you'd be up for that?"

"Today. Now." It was the first time we'd seen him excited for anything. It was hard to ignore.

The doc made a face. "I'll have to see if there's a warden or a nurse—"

"I'll take him," I said.

She looked at me then, and there was humour in her eyes. "You two aren't planning some great escape, are you? You're not gonna make a run for it?"

Justin smiled up at me, and I grinned right back at him. "We could . . ."

"But you won't," Doctor Chang said, stern but with a bit of a smile. "I'll see what I can find."

Two minutes later, she reappeared pushing a wheel-chair. Together, we helped Justin out of bed and into the chair. She got his leg propped up and properly supported, and I put a blanket over him. She gave us a list of instructions and warnings, but soon enough, I was pushing him out of his room.

I'm pretty sure I out-grinned him, but he was so much happier. "How about we go outside? It's sunny but it's not too hot, and there's a courtyard we—"

"Yes."

I chuckled and made our way to the exit. I ignored the way people stared at him, at the scar down the right side of his head, or how his right leg and right arm were clearly injured. I wanted to say, "Yeah, take a good look. This is what happens when half your body gets slammed by a fucking truck," but I thought better of it. I was proud of him for surviving, for coming this far.

I wheeled him out into the courtyard. There were flower beds and grass and a tree at the far end, but we only went to the grass. As soon as he was in direct sunlight, he closed his eyes and let his head fall back and let out an almighty sigh.

"Feel good?"

"So good." He smiled upward. "Never knew I'd miss this."

I wheeled him as close to the grass as I could. Then kneeling at his left side, I lifted his foot.

"What are you . . . ?"

I pushed the footrest up and gently lowered his good foot to the grass. "Can you feel that?"

"Oh."

I grinned up at him. "Feel good?"

He nodded. "Thank you."

He spread his toes a little and wiggled his foot in the grass, like he was planting himself in the earth. After weeks spent in a clinical ward, where everything was sterile and disposable, I imagined it felt amazing.

I parked my arse on the grass, stretched my legs out, leaned back on my hands, and turned my face to the sky. "Feels good, huh?"

"So good."

I chanced a look at him and found him with his face still turned skyward, a small smile at his lips. Christ, he was . . . everything to me.

Neither of us spoke for a bit and I wondered if he'd fallen asleep, but then he said, "The doctors gave me options for a home," he murmured quietly. "When I go . . . leave."

I sat upright, my heart strangled in my chest. "What?"

"Guess they had to. Needed to know I had options. But I told 'em I had a home." He brought his head forward and his eyes drew to mine. "You said I had a home?"

"You do." I nodded earnestly, trying not to let my panic show. "You do have a home."

"And a cat," he said like it was utterly absurd.

"Squish."

He nodded and then his face screwed up, a mix of pain and sadness. "I don't remember you," he whispered. "From before."

I swallowed hard, dreading what he was about to say. "I know."

He stared at me for a long, heart-stopping moment. "I wish I did. But I don't."

I tried to speak, but no words would come.

"Hey," he said, making me look at him. "It hurts you. I can see that."

I nodded again but didn't trust my voice to speak, if I could speak at all.

"But I trust you," he said quietly. "I dunno why."

I gave him a teary smile. "You used to say that before. That you felt safe with me. I know it was never easy for you to trust me. You had a shit time with guys in Darwin."

"I remember that."

"You moved back to Newcastle and said you weren't looking for a relationship, but then . . ." I let my words trail away.

"But I felt safe with you."

I nodded. "Yeah."

"Still do. It's hard to . . ." He squinted. "I forget my words . . ."

"It's hard to explain?" I guessed for him.

"Yeah. Explain. It's hard to explain. I don't know you, but I want to. I trust you. And there's . . ." He made a face. "Shit. My words."

"Take your time," I said gently. "There's no rush."

"The sun is starting to hurt my eyes," he said, squinting his eyes closed.

I jumped up. "Okay, then let's get you somewhere else."

I fixed his footrest and wheeled him back inside, and we just walked slowly for a bit. "Want to check out the cafeteria?"

"Sure."

"Just tell me if you've had enough or if you want to go back," I said, not wanting him to overdo it. We'd only been out for half an hour, but still. "How's your headache?"

"'S okay."

When he said okay, he meant ever-present, never-subsiding, skull-crushing pain. The drugs took the edge off, of course, but it was always there. I could tell when he hurt in particular, as his right eye would sag a little or he'd squint more often.

"Did you want something to eat or drink?" I asked as we neared the cafeteria.

"Um . . . I dunno."

"What about some fries? Just a small one, between us. Then I better get you back, or Doctor Chang will send out a search party."

He seemed happy enough as we waited for our order, but his blinks were getting a little heavy. "People look at me," he said.

"Maybe they want to see a guy who survived getting hit by a truck," I said jokingly. "He's pretty great."

He smiled but it faded fast. "Don't feel it."

"Well, you are." I leaned in closer. "And fuck anyone who stares. They don't know what you've been through or how far you've come."

That earned me a small smile, but then our fries came and he savoured the first taste. "Real food."

I laughed. "If the doctors asked, tell them I bought you salad." He'd lost some weight in the first two weeks after his accident, but he was starting to fill out again. The iced coffees probably had something to do with that.

"Calm," he said.

"What? Calm, what?"

"The word I couldn't say," he replied. "Before. I lost the word. Calm, that's it."

"What's calm?" I couldn't remember . . .

"You. Me. You make me feel calm. I trust you. I dunno why. But I'm calm when you're here."

I had to swallow the lump in my throat. "Thank you."

"So when I go home," he said, slow blinking, almost asleep. "I go with you."

CHAPTER SEVEN

FOR THE NEXT FEW DAYS, Justin wanted to escape his room in the wheelchair and I was all too happy to oblige. He had the staples in his leg removed, he did his physio, and he was eating more. He still became exhausted easily, he still forgot some words when he was tired, and he still had splitting headaches. The doc said these things could, and probably would, take weeks or months to abate. Maybe even longer.

And that was okay with me. I was here for the long haul. I was in it for forever before his accident, and I wasn't the type to quit when things got tough. Certainly not when he needed me the most.

When I got back to the hospital after the mandatory midday rest period, he was still asleep. He'd been looking through the photos again because they were in a messy pile, and the deck of cards I'd brought in for him was on his table as well.

Each and every visit was different, and I never knew what I'd be walking into. Would he be in a good mood? Would he be unwell? Would he be angry and frustrated or sore from pushing himself too hard? Would he be more tired than usual? Or would he be itching to get out of his room again?

Him being asleep, or dozing at least, wasn't too unusual. Exhaustion and constant tiredness were common after a brain injury, and I thought nothing of it. I planted my back-side into my seat and answered a few emails on my phone that I hadn't got to yet.

Justin began to stir . . . No, not stir awake. He was still sound asleep. He was having a nightmare. He began to twitch and mumble in his sleep, slow at first but then urgent and a little scary. His face etched in pain and his body jerked, his mumbling growing frantic.

He was going to hurt his arm or reopen the scars on his leg.

I took his hand. "Hey, Justin," I soothed. "Hey, baby."

He jerked again and groaned as though something hurt. I stood up and put my hand to his cheek. "Jusso, it's okay. Wake up. I'm here with you."

His eyes shot open, wild and unseeing, until the pain kicked in and he moaned as he sagged back on the bed. "It was just a dream," I whispered. "You're okay. You're safe here."

He let out a shaky breath, his eyes closed, and he shook his head. "Fuck."

I gave him a few seconds to take some deep breaths and collect himself. "Just a bad dream," I murmured.

When he was calmer and breathing easier, I asked, "Do you remember what your dream was about?"

His fingers gripped mine and I noticed his strength was definitely returning, and after a long while, he shook his head. "No."

I suspected he might have nightmares about the accident, and I didn't know if I was disappointed that he still couldn't remember it or if I was glad he couldn't.

I wanted him to remember something.

Anything.

He kept his eyes closed while he concentrated on his breathing, and he eventually let go of my hand so he could sit himself up a bit more. "Hurts when I get like that," he mumbled.

"All tense?" I asked, and he nodded. "You jerked your injured leg and your broken arm. That has to hurt."

He made a face. "Yeah."

"Can I get you anything? A drink of juice or water? Did you need me to get the nurse?"

He shook his head and closed his eyes again. "Just sit with me."

There he was again, saying things to make my heart go crazy. "Of course."

He was quiet for a long few moments, and I sat beside him with my hand on his arm. "I don't like the dreams," he said eventually. "I dunno if it's my brain remembering something. It's hard to know what's real."

I frowned, my heart hurting for him. "Can you remember the dream? Maybe I can help shed some light . . ." I didn't know what else to say.

He turned his head slowly and stared at me. "Not really. It's like I'm falling. It's dark. Nothing is . . ." He licked his lips and sighed. "Kinda feels like I'm gonna die."

I slid my hand down his arm and took his hand, threading our fingers. "That sounds awful. I wish I could make them stop. The dreams, that is. It's probably just your brain trying to process what it's been through. Hopefully they'll stop or become clearer."

He almost smiled. "Hopefully. I have another dream

too, but I can't quite remember . . . It's hard to know what's real."

"Is there anything you remember from that one?"

He closed his eyes as though he was trying to recapture it. "I don't know."

"That's okay. Don't try to force it." I could see it was an uneasy topic, so I changed it. "So, the occupational therapist came by," I said. I'd told him the appointment was today but didn't expect him to remember the details. "To check the flat and see if we'd need to change or fix anything before you come home."

"Oh yeah? What'd they say?"

"Everything's fine. Except for the stairs. The flat's above the shop. The mechanic shop, so the stairs are gonna be a pain until your leg is better. Just means you'll have to go slow, one step at a time. But everything else is fine. I thought the shower might be a pain for you, but she said it was great. I mean, it's only a two-bedroom unit, and it ain't too fancy, but I guess simple is good. No trip hazards or nothing, so that's good."

He nodded slowly and his brow furrowed a bit. "Stairs . . ."

"Yeah, Davo and Sparra were gonna try and rig up some kind of crank seat, like with a really big bike chain, and if they used an old two-stroke motor . . ." I shook my head. "I think the lady thought they were joking."

He did smile at that. "Davo and Sparra. I know them, right?"

"Yep. You've worked with them since you came back to Newcastle." I took the pile of photos and found the one of them and pointed each of them out. "That's Davo, and that's Sparra."

"Is that his name? Sparra?"

"Nah, his last name is Bird. Tony Bird is his real name, but apparently when he was in high school, Bird became sparrow, and well, sparrow became Sparra."

Justin's smile widened. "And I like them, right?"

"You sure do. They're great guys. Davo's basically been running the shop for me. I'll owe him a few cartons of beer, I reckon."

Justin's eyes met mine. "You don't have to come in every day."

"Yes I do," I replied. "Of course I do. I don't want to be anywhere else. Unless you'd rather I didn't, but I'll be here until you say otherwise."

He rested his head on the mattress, but his gaze never left mine. He just stared for a while, and I wanted so bad to lean in and kiss him. I wanted it so, so bad. But those days were gone . . .

"Sucks that you gotta look after me," he mumbled. "Like I'm a kid or something."

"It won't be forever. You'll be up on your feet in no time." I put my hand back on his, which he didn't seem to mind. "And it's no hassle. You don't owe me anything, no apologies, nothing. I do this because . . ." I paused because I almost said something that maybe he wasn't ready for. But then I realised maybe he needed to know. "Because I love you, Justin. Years ago, I made a promise to you to be by your side through whatever life threw at us. I know you don't remember, but you don't have to. Because I remember. And I'll be by your side for as long as you'll have me."

He stared for a few heartbeats and he opened his mouth to speak, just as there was a soft knock on his door.

It was two uniformed police officers, oblivious to the moment me and Justin were having, and the first had a clear plastic bag with them. "Sorry to interrupt," the first cop said. He offered Justin a smile. "You're looking a lot better than the last time I saw you."

Justin stared blankly, then he looked at me. I shrugged.

The cop explained. "I was one of the first on the scene of your accident. I helped get you out of the van."

I got to my feet and offered my hand to shake. "Thank you."

"Had some personal items from evidence I thought you might like returned." He held the plastic bag out to me. I could see it was Justin's wallet and his phone and what looked like some papers and a logbook, so I put it on Justin's table. "They were in the van at the time of the accident. We don't need them, and I thought I'd save you the trip down to the station."

"Uh, thanks," Justin said.

He'd been questioned very early on but, of course, couldn't remember anything. Those first few days, he really wasn't in shape to be questioned at all.

"Still can't remember anything?" the second cop asked. It wasn't meant to be callous, but Jesus Christ, some empathy wouldn't have hurt.

Justin gave a small shake of his head. "No."

I gave the second cop a curt smile. "He can't remember anything from the last five years. Not one thing."

"Yeah, sorry," he replied sheepishly.

"What happened to the driver?" Justin asked.

Whether it was because Justin spoke slow and a little slurred or the first cop felt bad or not, I couldn't be sure, but he seemed to take some pity on Justin. "He wasn't injured, if that's what you mean. There was dashcam footage, and he returned a negative for drugs and alcohol. It's been ruled as an accident. His brakes locked up in the rain. There were a lot of witnesses." His voice softened, like he slipped out of police-mode. "He's actually pretty shaken up about it, and he's very sorry. He wanted to come see you but was advised against it. He knows you were badly injured."

Justin slow blinked, and I could almost hear his brain catching up with everything the cop just said. "He can come see me," he said. "I don' mind."

"You sure?" I asked Justin.

He gave a nod, but he closed his eyes and sighed.

I looked at the policemen and tilted my chin toward the door, and they followed me out. "He gets tired real easy," I explained quietly. "And today hasn't been a great day."

"Sorry," the first cop said, and I believed him. He seemed genuine and I liked him. "For what it's worth, I'm glad he made it. I had my doubts when I first saw him in that van, but he's obviously a fighter."

I nodded, unsure if I was about to cry or laugh. "Thanks for coming by," I managed.

"I'll let the driver of the truck know," he said. "He's an older guy, been driving trucks for forty years and never had so much as a parking fine. He's really struggling, mentally and emotionally."

He's not the only one, I thought.

"Anyway, I'll pass on the message but will be sure he gives adequate notice of a visit," he said. "Who knows, it might help them both."

I nodded. "Maybe. Mornings are better. He's not so tired. And tell him no flowers on the neuro ward," I added. "The staff wouldn't let them in anyway, so just to save him the money . . ."

"I'll be sure to pass that on," he said. "Thanks again." He clapped my shoulder and they left, and I went back into Justin's room.

I thought he was asleep, but his eyelids opened slowly. "They go?"

I smiled. "Yeah. Said to say thanks." I sat back next to him. "If you don't want that truck driver here, if you change your mind, you just let me know."

He sighed and looked wearily at me. "I dunno . . . I think I need to see him. Dunno. My life was okay up to . . . what I remember last. Then it's gone. Like blank. Like a puzzle with no pieces. I need any pieces I can get."

I let out a long, sad breath and gave his hand a squeeze. He gripped my fingers and held my hand, and I relished the feel of his skin against mine, the warmth of it that seeped through to my core, because I wasn't just holding his hand— he was holding mine.

"Looks like they brought you your wallet and phone," I said eventually, nodding toward the bag on his table.

He reluctantly let go of my hand and reached for the bag. He opened it with one hand and tipped the contents out. He took his phone first and pressed the button on the bottom. It was dead, unsurprisingly. "Screen's cracked," he noted.

"It was cracked before the accident," I said. "You dropped it on the concrete floor at the shop."

He huffed. "Course I did."

"I can bring your charger in tomorrow," I said. I would have offered to take it home and charge it overnight, but I didn't want him to think I'd delete anything . . . not that I thought he would think that, but I didn't want him to wonder or question. I wanted to be as transparent as I could be.

He took his wallet next, opening it and sliding his licence out. He inspected it, and I supposed it must have felt like he'd found something from the future. But it was his photo, our address, and the date. He took out the bank card, his Medicare card, other membership cards, but he clearly didn't recognise them. He pulled out the two twenty-dollar notes and shrugged. "Should probably give this to you," he said. "For the iced coffees."

I laughed as he slid something else out of his wallet. It was a photograph, and one I'd forgotten was in there. It was of him and me with our arms around each other, dressed up in our good jeans and shirts, smiling at the camera. He stared at it and stared some more. He frowned and shook his head, clearly drawing a blank.

"We were going to a concert," I said quietly. "I got you tickets to see Birds of Tokyo for your birthday, two years ago."

His gaze went to mine. "I wish I could remember . . ."

"I know you do."

He shook his head. "No. I really do." He thumbed the photograph. "It's like I'm looking at a stranger. Like I'm looking at photos of people I've never met. Even me. I don't recognise me in this . . ." He frowned again, his eyes teary. "I look so happy. And I don't remember . . . I feel . . . cheated. Like this was taken away from me." A tear escaped and he wiped it away with the back of his hand and stared at the photo. "All I ever wanted was . . . this."

"And you have it," I replied, swallowing back my own tears. *What else could I say?* "I'm not going anywhere, Juss. We can get back to this. If you never remember anything, it's okay. We'll make new memories. You're very loved by everyone. You'll have it again."

He closed his eyes again, tears beading on his eyelashes. "I want to remember," he whispered.

"I know you do."

His eyes stayed closed and his breathing deepened. I

thought he'd gone back to sleep, but when I tried to let go of his hand, he gripped it tighter. "Stay. Talk to me. I like your voice."

I couldn't help but smile. "I like your voice too."

He smiled and ducked his head, but then he slowly rolled onto his side to face me. Something he rarely did because of his injuries, but I helped pull his pillow under his head to support his neck more and waited for him to get comfortable.

"Did you want me to read to you?" I asked.

"No," he whispered. "Tell me how we met."

Oh.

My heart danced around in my chest and I damn near could have cried. Somehow I held it together enough to speak. "You applied for a job at my shop. Of course I hired you because you're one of the best mechanics I'd ever seen. You'd just moved back from Darwin and you were keen for the work." I smiled fondly at the memory. "You were also scorching hot and funny. You were kind and gentle-natured, and apparently I used to not be able to speak around you. Davo took the piss out of me for months, because every time you walked in, I was utterly useless. But I didn't know if you were into guys, and I had this 'don't get involved with work-mates' policy that I'd managed to abide by for a decade."

Justin's eyes were heavy-lidded, but he was smiling.

"And anyway, Davo reckoned you'd been checking me out, and one day when we were both there, he asked you if you were seeing anyone, a girl or a guy. I could have killed him," I said with a laugh. "But anyway, you said you didn't have a boyfriend, and he said something like, 'Oh, that's a coincidence because neither does Dallas.' Like he just put it all on the table in front of us, ya know?"

Justin kept smiling.

"Then after more weeks of us dancing around each other—not being able to be in the same room as each other, basically—Davo locked us both in my office and told us the sexual tension was unbearable and we weren't coming out until either one of us quit or we finally made out."

He slow blinked. "He locked us in your office?"

I nodded. "Yep."

"One of us didn't quit, did we?"

I shook my head slowly. "Uh, no." My laughter became a sigh. "We didn't come out of my office for a while either."

He made a happy sound. Though his eyes were closed now, he was still smiling. "Davo sounds like a good guy."

I chuckled. "He reminded us all the time that we owed our relationship to him. When we decided on the boyfriend thing, then again when you moved in with me, and again when we decided to become cat-dads and keep Squish. Now that I think about it, Davo's actually been a bit of a dick about it, to be honest. But yeah, he's a good guy."

He never opened his eyes, but he seemed so peaceful, happy even. "Tell me more," he mumbled. And I would have, but he was already asleep.

CHAPTER EIGHT

THE NEXT DAY I arrived with Justin's phone charger and plugged his phone in while he took his first sip of iced coffee. It was gonna take a little while for the battery to come to life, but he didn't seem to mind. He was in a good mood today.

He'd been going through his daily exercises, and he said he'd even been up and peed by himself. He was proud and I was chuckling when there was a knock at the door. Amy, the nurse, appeared and came in hesitantly. "Justin, there's a gentleman here to see you. Apparently he'd asked if he could see you and you said yes. He was driving the truck," she said with a frown. "If you don't want to see him, that's okay. I'm sure he'll understand."

"No, it's okay," Justin said. He looked at me, his eyes asking something I couldn't read. "You'll stay?"

"Yeah, of course. If you want me to stay, then yes."

He let out a breath and nodded at Amy. "I'll bring him in," she said before disappearing out the door.

"You sure?" I asked Justin.

He swallowed hard. "Yep. I don't know why, but I think

I need to do this." But then he held out his hand to me and I was stunned for a second, wondering what he might have meant or wanted, but when I slid my hand over his, he clasped onto it.

Of course it made my insides all warm, but there was no time to savour it. An older man with grey hair and grey eyebrows stepped inside, wringing his hands. He looked on the verge of tears, and I'd wondered if he'd slept at all. "Good morning," he said. "The name's Jimmy Litchfield. I was . . ." His voice broke. His eyes were glassy. "I was driving the truck that hit your van. I just wanted you to know how sorry I am, and how . . . well, yeah. How very sorry I am."

I turned to Justin and he squeezed my hand. "Hey, Jimmy, I'm Justin."

I stood up and let go of Justin's hand so I could offer my hand to Jimmy. "I'm Dallas," I said without adding a title or point of reference to my being there or holding Justin's hand. The fact was, Justin and I weren't really boyfriends anymore . . . I mean, my heart still thought so, but my brain knew I couldn't be boyfriends with someone who didn't know me. "Please come in," I said to Jimmy, gesturing to the other side of the bed. I sat back down and took Justin's hand once more.

"The nice policeman said I could come see you and that mornings were best," Jimmy said. "I've been . . . I've been a bit of a mess since the accident." He then gestured to Justin lying in the hospital bed. "Not as much as you. That's not what I meant. I just meant . . ."

"It's okay," Justin said. "I get it."

"I can't stop thinking about it, and I don't sleep much anymore," Jimmy said. "It was an accident and the truck locked up on me. I hit the water and just aquaplaned straight into ya." He frowned deeper than I thought possible. "I can still see your face as I was coming for ya. I tried to stop . . ."

"I don't remember the accident," Justin said.

"The policeman said you lost your memory," Jimmy said.

"Five years," Justin said quietly. "Like someone just erased it."

"That's just awful," he said, getting teary again. "I'm real sorry. I know sorry don't mean much."

"Yeah it does," Justin said. "It helps that you came to see me. I need as many pieces as I can get."

Jimmy nodded, but I doubted he understood what Justin meant. "And your leg and arm . . . ?"

"Yeah, got myself some hardware," Justin said, looking at his leg with the brace. "New suspension rig."

Jimmy managed a smile. "Can see that."

"And my arm's not too bad. Looks worse than it is." Justin put his head back and managed a smile. "Head's not as hard as I thought it was though. Well, the thick skull was finally good for something, but the inside got . . . shook a bit."

"Despite all his injuries," I added, smiling at Justin, "we were still very lucky."

Jimmy looked at me then, and he saw our hands joined. It took him a second to recover, but he did it well. "My wife drove me in today. I'm still not good behind the wheel," he said. "Bit too jittery, since the accident, that is. And I'd be lost without her. Real good woman. And I'm glad you got someone here with you too. I can't imagine if you didn't have someone." He was teary again and got choked up. "My granddaughter married a nice girl. Real smart and takes good care of my girl, and that's all I ever wanted for her. So I just wanted you to know. That I don't care about this." He waved at our joined hands. "I voted yes to marriage equality because it's a good thing." He grimaced as though he was horrified at his verbal diarrhoea.

Justin snorted quietly, then turned to me, his eyes wide. "Wait. Marriage what?"

I laughed and gave his hand a squeeze. "Marriage equality. I'll explain that later." Jimmy looked all kinds of confused, so I clarified. "He can't remember that. The last five years is gone."

"Oh, sorry," Jimmy said, frowning again. "I guess . . . the last five years, right."

"There's a lot he needs to get caught up on," I said, smiling at Justin.

Justin nodded. "Sounds like it." Then he lifted his head up. "Wait. Did the Knights win a premiership in the last five years?"

I laughed, and Jimmy broke out in a grin. "No, son," he said. "You haven't missed that."

Jimmy stayed for a few minutes more, and he really was a nice old fella. He genuinely felt terrible, and the cops were right. Both Justin and Jimmy needed this. Jimmy needed to know that Justin was okay, and Justin needed to see the human aspect of the accident that took so much from him. Not to blame anyone, but to see that it was an accident and nothing more. And maybe that feeling of disbelief, that awful doubt, the not knowing that was now Justin's reality, might get a little closure.

I walked Jimmy out and saw him to the end of the ward. "Will he be okay?" Jimmy asked. "He talks slow. Did he used to talk like that, you know . . . before?"

I shook my head. "No, he didn't used to talk like that. But he's getting better every day. He doesn't forget words too much anymore, and he's really improving. The docs said he's real lucky. He might not ever remember the last five years though," I answered.

"Well, at least he has you. I'm glad he remembers you."

I tried to smile. "He, uh, he doesn't remember me. Not from before. He only knows me as the guy who hasn't left since he woke up."

Jimmy stared, and this time a tear did escape. He blinked and wiped at his face. "I'm so sorry. I never was one to pray, but I've been asking the good Lord to watch over him."

I was the least religious person on the planet and Justin was one step behind me. "I'm really grateful for that. You keep those prayers coming, okay?"

He nodded and wiped at his face again, just as an older woman wearing a blue sundress came down the hallway. Jimmy saw her and he began to cry again. Her face softened and she took his arm. "Thank you for seeing us today," she said. "It means a lot to my Jimmy."

"No problem." They turned to leave, but I didn't want to end it like this. This poor man was really struggling. "Hey, Jimmy," I called out and waited for him to turn. "We have the bike shop, Muller's Mechanics on Carney Road."

"I know it."

"Well, that's us. I'm Dallas Muller." I gave him a smile. "How 'bout you give me a call in a few weeks and I'll let you know how he's getting on. Or you could even drop by and see him, but call me first."

It felt strange to be making plans for weeks or months ahead when I didn't even know what tomorrow would bring, but it felt right.

"I'd really like that," Jimmy said, finally smiling. "I'll do that." He gave a determined, thankful nod, and I'd like to think I gave him some light in what had been a dark few weeks for him.

I watched them walk away, and with a deep sigh, I went back to Justin's room. He was on the bed, of course, but he was lifting his sore leg, doing his exercises. "His wife met us in the hall," I said.

"He was a nice fella," Justin said.

"He was. He's a bit upset. I think it did him good to see you," I said. "How do you feel now?"

"Better, I think." He shrugged his good shoulder. "I'd be pissed if it was a drunk driver or a stolen car or something. Or if he didn't care. Ya know? Like if he changed my whole life and didn't give a fuck." Then he grimaced. "Sorry. Do we swear?"

I laughed. "Ah, yeah. We do. Probably too much. Just not in front of customers."

Justin smirked. "Got it."

"But you feel better now that you've met him?"

He nodded and chewed on his bottom lip for a bit. "I didn't want the accident . . ." He cleared his throat. "The nightmares I have. The darkness and the fear. I dunno if it's my brain trying to show me the accident, to tell me what went wrong, ya know? But now it's not so scary. It's just a nice old guy whose brakes locked up in the rain. It wasn't . . ."

I frowned. "It wasn't what?"

"It wasn't death driving that truck."

I stared at him.

"That sounds stupid, sorry," he added quickly. "I dunno why I think that. It's just a stupid dream."

I took his hand in both of mine, sitting beside him. "Hey, it's not stupid. It doesn't sound stupid. It sounds pretty fucking real, if you ask me. It's no wonder those nightmares scare the shit out of you. And I'm sorry you've carried that around with you."

He sighed, frowning. "Maybe now I've met the driver, it won't be so bad."

I nodded. "Let's hope so."

I was going to ask if he had the nightmares every night, or even about the other dream he'd mentioned, when there was a light knock at the door. "Ugh, PT time," he mumbled.

While Justin was expecting his physical therapist, instead he was met by his other doctors. Doctor Chang gave him a big smile. "Good morning," she said cheerfully. "I have some good news!"

"Uh, okay," Justin hedged, unsure.

"I think you're ready to go home," she said. "The last MRI and tests came back and I'm happy with the results, and Doctor Anderson is too. We still want to run a few more physical tests, but I think we can move onto the next step in your recovery. And that involves going home."

Justin was speechless, and I couldn't work out if it was a good speechless or a bad one.

"When?" I asked.

"We want to see how he goes with some mobility aids today, and all things going well, you can bust him maybe even tomorrow." She went on to explain a few things about home care services and whatever, but my concern was Justin.

I took his hand. "Hey," I said quietly. He looked at me. "Are you okay with that? With going home? Do you think you're ready?"

He swallowed hard. "I want to be ready," he replied. "But I . . ."

He was scared. Not just about being on his own, but he was scared about leaving with a man he didn't really know.

"How about this?" I said, trying to be braver than I felt. "We'll get you home and settled in. The home care nurse will come by every other day, and if you'd prefer to stay somewhere else, you just have to tell them. And we'll figure it out. No pressure, okay?"

He let out a breath and looked to his lap. Then he nodded. "I want to leave here, but I don't know what or where home is."

Doctor Chang intervened. "Going home will be a huge adjustment for you, and you can expect to be off-kilter and feeling a little lost and confused. It's not going to be easy, but I think you're ready for it. I wouldn't suggest it otherwise."

Then the occupational therapist stepped closer to the bed. I hadn't even noticed before but she was wheeling some kind of scooter thing that had four small wheels, a bike seat, and handlebars like the scooters the kids of today rode. "This is a steerable seated scooter," she said, then she proceeded to sit on it and prop her right foot up on a footrest above the front wheel. "You can steer with one hand and propel yourself with your left foot."

She wanted Justin to try it. Crutches were no good because the cast on his arm went up to his armpit, and a wheelchair wasn't much use when he couldn't use his right arm to help push himself. But this scooter with a seat should be good for him and would hopefully allow him to reclaim some of his independence around the flat.

He sat himself up and gently lowered his right leg to the floor. He took a few moments to let his head catch up with being upright, and when he was certain he was ready, we helped him onto it. The doc put his right foot up onto the footrest and allowed another few seconds to let him find his equilibrium. He leaned his bandaged right arm on his lap, but he gripped the handlebar with his left like a pro.

"We might be able to rig up a motor," I joked. "Just a two-stroke, or a Peewee 50—"

The two doctors and one nurse all spun to yell at me. "No!"

But Justin laughed. He actually laughed, and so help me God, he looked at me and my heart soared.

Doctor Chang could see it was a joke, and I was pretty sure she liked seeing Justin happy, but she was still a doctor. "It's a mobility aid, not a motocross bike. There will be no modifications to the scooter. Are we clear? Accidents are one thing, but I charge double for stupidity."

"No modifications," I said with a grin. "Got it."

All jokes aside, they helped Justin move the scooter, standing either side of him in case he fell or became dizzy. But he could do it, and his smile when he turned around in the hallway told me everything I needed to know.

He was ready.

He was coming home.

WHEN I CAME BACK after the lunchtime rest period, he was scrolling through his phone. He put it down on his lap when I came in and gave me a look I couldn't quite decipher. He looked tired, but there was something else . . . I held up the overnight bag. "Clothes for going home," I said, putting the bag by his bed.

"Thanks," he said, but he chewed on his bottom lip like he wanted to say something but didn't know how.

"Hey," I said gently. "Everything okay?"

"Yeah, just." He picked his phone back up. "Just looking through this."

"Find anything?"

"Well, lots. Nothing I remember. But you're in here. A lot, actually."

I sat in my seat and gave him a smile. "Photos, I take it. And texts."

He nodded and scrolled, though I couldn't see the screen.

"Is that weird?" I asked.

"A bit," he answered. "Like I'm reading texts between strangers. I should . . ." He sighed. "I should feel something, but I don't. Not like that. It just makes me feel sad."

"Sad?"

"Because it's all missing. This life." He turned the phone around, and I could see a text conversation. He read it aloud to me. "You: *Still at Coles?* Me: *Yep.* You: *We're out of milk.* Me: *Okay.*" He looked at me then. "It's just so . . ."

"Boring? Unromantic?" I prompted.

He snorted. "I was gonna say nice. Like it's so real life and normal."

I smiled because that was true. But it was also kinda sad because all he'd ever wanted was normal. He'd never wanted anything fancy or a high-flying, dramatic romance. Just a boyfriend to be at home with. Sure, we had our own romance, but we were two blokey blokes whose idea of together-time was riding and fixing motorbikes. "It was."

He scrolled some more. "And here," he said, showing me the screen. "Me: *Hey babe, running late. Be home soon.* You: *Okay, drive safe.* Me: *Want me to get KFC for dinner?* You: *Do I get a choice?* Me: *Nope. KFC it is.* With a laughing face."

I chuckled. "You like KFC."

He sighed as he stared at the screen. "And the photos."

"Oh . . ." I made a face. "Were there any nudes? I probably should have paid more attention to the photos you kept."

He turned the phone around and showed me the screen, giving me a flat stare. "I can't see if we're fully naked in this, but that's me on a bed and I think that's your arm, and I'm fairly certain I know what we're doing."

I laughed, my cheeks heating. "Uh, yeah. I took that photo. I was telling you how hot you were when we—" I cleared my throat. "—when we made love, and I took a photo to show you. I didn't know you kept it. You were supposed to delete it."

He let out a breath. "I take it I still . . . I mean, I always liked to . . ." He shook his head. "Never mind."

"If you have any questions, about anything, I will do my best to answer you. I'm trying to keep my emotional response out of it and just answer with facts so I don't colour the information with my experience. Which isn't easy." I shrugged. "But don't be embarrassed. You can ask me anything. I'm trying to help you."

He made a face. "I was just going to say that I always liked to . . . bottom," he whispered, "and from this photo . . ."

"If you're asking if you bottomed and I topped, then ah, yeah. You did."

His cheeks were red. "Well, at least that's something that hasn't changed."

I laughed, but I didn't want to dwell on the sexual side of us. I didn't want him to feel pressured, and if—if, one day —it ever happened again, it would happen when he was ready. "Any other photos?"

He sighed again. "Lots. There's a lot of bikes. That also

hasn't changed. There's pictures of a cat being all cute and shit."

I chuckled. "Squish."

"How did we get him?"

"We found three abandoned kittens at the shop. You made a bed for them and left food out for the mum cat, but she never came back. So you started feeding them and looking after them. Davo and Sparra thought you were crazy, but you were determined. Anyway, you had the vet check them over and you found homes for two of them, but no one wanted the black cat. Bad luck or some bullshit. Not that it mattered because there was no way you were giving him up anyway. We kept saying you should have called him Shadow because he was always one step behind you, but you called him Squish."

"I named him that?"

"Yep. You kept saying you were gonna squish him if he didn't get out from under your feet."

Justin smiled. "That's kinda cute."

"It's totally cute. He misses you," I added. "Squish does. He yells at me when you don't come through the door with me."

Still smiling, he went back to his phone. "There's a bunch of pictures of those two guys, Davo and Sparra. Mostly goofing around. It's a mechanic workshop, so I guess it's where I worked too?"

I nodded slowly. "Yep. That's the one."

"And there's pictures of you and me, but mostly you, and even of the cat that's in a house. The walls and furniture are the same."

"That's the flat above the workshop," I explained. "That's where you live."

"Thought so." He scrolled through a few more photos. "Are there any posters in our flat?"

"Posters?" I shook my head. "Like wall posters? No, we weren't big on decorating, if that's what you mean. Why, do you remember something?"

"I don't know. I see something in my dream. I think it's a poster."

"A poster of what?"

He made a face. "Of a Harley Davidson. So weird, I know. But it's hard to focus on and I'm not sure."

I shook my head slowly. "No, sorry. Was there one in your place in Darwin?"

He shook his head and frowned, then let the phone screen go dark and laid it on his lap, resting his head back on the pillow. He let out a long sigh. "You know it's weird, but I know how to use a phone, and I remember how to ride a bike, but I can't remember where I live or who I live with. I can't remember my friends, but I can remember how to make my nan's spaghetti. The doc gave it some big fancy name, but to me, it's just weird."

It was called procedural memory function, but I didn't need to rub that in his face right now. The name wasn't the important part of this story. "It is weird, Justin. The skills are there, like how to do stuff, but the facts and info are gone."

He nodded. "Yep. Doc told you too, huh?"

I smirked. "Yep."

"She said going home can trigger some memories." Justin's speech was getting slower, a sure sign he was tired. "Like if I see the cat, I'll get *bam, bam, bam,* flashes of me getting the cat, feeding the cat, cuddling the cat. She said sometimes that happens, but not always."

"Well, we can hope."

He slow blinked. "It's like right there. In the mist. But right there."

"What's right there?"

"Memories," he mumbled. "Everything. Like I can almost touch 'em but can't."

He could barely keep his eyes open, so I took his hand, and the familiar warmth was incredible. "Have a nap, Juss," I whispered. "You need all the rest you can get. Got a busy day tomorrow."

His eyes stayed closed but he gave a small smile. "Leaving."

It stung a little that he didn't say 'going home,' but to be fair, it wasn't home to him. But I was going to do my damnedest to make it his home again.

"Yeah, baby," I whispered, knowing he was already asleep. "Leaving."

CHAPTER NINE

WHEN I ARRIVED the next morning, Justin was sitting up on the edge of his bed, showered and dressed. I'd chosen some loose track pants for him, thinking they'd be easier on his leg, and one of his favourite shirts. He looked so different in normal clothes rather than the hospital garb he'd been in for the last three and a half weeks.

"Morning," I said, unable to hide my excitement. "How are you feeling?"

He smiled. "Okay. Nervous."

"I'm nervous too," I admitted.

"You are?"

"Sure. I'm nervous that I might not be the best home care person and you'll hurt yourself because I did something wrong."

"Like what?"

"I dunno. Leave the bathmat on the floor and you'll trip over it and smack your head on the tub. Or that the stairs are gonna be too much for you. That kind of thing."

Or that you'll realise you don't want to live with me anymore . . .

"That makes two of us," he murmured.

"You're worried that I'll be a bad home carer?"

He snorted. "Uh, no. I'm worried that you *have* to be my home carer, that you'll get sick of having to babysit me."

I went to him and stood in front of him, putting my hand on his shoulder. "I'll never get sick of it. You're not a burden, and you're not a hassle. We'll get through this. It just means you'll have to put up with my terrible cooking for a bit."

He almost smiled. "Thanks." But then he took a deep breath and met my gaze. "I mean it. Thank you. You don't have to do this, like you could have bailed, but you didn't. I could have had no recollection of my life before the accident and be homeless. But you stuck by me."

My hand burned to touch his face, to cup his cheek so I could kiss him softly. Of course I couldn't, so I pulled my hand away. "I wouldn't be anywhere else." He smiled but looked away. A line formed between his eyebrows. "How's your arm feel? Is that shirt okay?" I'd chosen one with loose short sleeves.

He looked down and lifted his arm out a little. "Yeah, thanks. It's fine. They re-bandaged it. Doc was happy with it."

"Good. Did they say when you can leave?"

"Just waiting for the doc to come by. She's got papers and pills, that kinda stuff."

"Okay. Did you eat already? I put your iced coffee in the fridge at home. Thought it might be something to look forward to."

He smiled more genuinely then. "Thanks. Yeah, I had some toast."

I pointed my chin at the scooter seat thing. "Wanna give

it a whirl? I mean, we gotta get used to it with just me helping you."

His smile widened. "Okay. Yeah, okay."

I wheeled it so it was in front of him and put the brakes on, then went to his left side and took his arm. "So," I said. "All your weight on your good foot. Ready?"

He gave a nod, his face etched in concentration. "Yep."

He stood, and holding him with one hand, I manoeuvred the scooter back so he could lower himself onto the seat. We wobbled a bit but we held steady, and I lifted his right foot up onto the footrest. I looked up at him to find him grinning. "We good?" I asked.

"We're good." He was panting a little, but he'd come so far from the first time he'd used this.

Yes, we were. We were gonna be just fine.

"Oh, I see someone's keen?" Doctor Chang said from the door. She was smiling, holding a folder and a white paper bag.

"Oh," I said, feeling like a kid getting in trouble. "We just thought we'd see if we could get him onto it without another significant head trauma incident."

The doc stared at me but Justin laughed, and she relented with a sigh and a bit of a smile. "Well, I'm glad there was not another traumatic brain injury. Because one is enough." She put the folder on Justin's bed and asked him to wheel over. She showed him his release forms, every prescription he needed, an itinerary of all his follow-up appointments, exercise and physio stuff, and a booklet journal for him to document anything and everything. She then showed us his pill schedule, which was an entire freaking chemist full—pills for pain, anti-seizure, anti-inflammatory, anti-coagulants, and whatever else— and I was so glad it was all written down. She closed the folder. "It's a lot of information."

I nodded but gave Justin an encouraging smile. "We got this. Once we get home and find our own routine, we'll have it down pat."

Doctor Chang gave me a fond look. "Yes, you will."

A nurse came in with a wheelchair. "Your ride, sir."

"Can't I leave on this?" he asked Doctor Chang.

"Sorry. Hospital policy."

"I'm more of a fall-risk when I get out of the chair and onto this thing," he tried.

"Mr Keith," Doctor Chang said. "Please humour me."

He sighed. "You know, I can remember high school. And being called that reminds me a lot of high school."

I laughed and Doctor Chang shook her head. "You two," she said, rolling her eyes.

But like a good boy, I helped Justin transfer to the wheelchair, and the nurse took him out to the station to say a round of goodbyes. Doctor Chang stayed beside me. "He was very lucky in that accident," she said quietly. "It could have been a lot worse than what it was. But it's not all going to be easy. There's going to be hard roads ahead."

"I know," I said. "But we've got this."

"He's lucky to have you," she whispered before she met my eyes. She breathed in deep and gave me a watery smile. "I wish I could tell you he'll regain his memories, but I can't."

I gave a nod. I knew this too; if he hadn't regained anything after six months, it wasn't likely he ever would. "Yeah. We'll just have to make new ones."

She looked at me like she was trying to figure something out. "You can't be shaken, can you?"

I almost laughed. Because, Jesus, this whole accident

had shaken me to my core. "Quite the opposite actually. But what choice do I have? He might not remember me, but he needs me. And I love him."

She nodded, her eyes glassy. "I wish every one of my patients had a you."

The nurse wheeled Justin back to us. He looked up at Doctor Chang. "Well, Doc. It's been fun."

"But you can't wait to leave me," she said, joking. She nodded toward the exit. "Well, you can't get rid of me that easy. I'm walking you out."

I put Justin's overnight bag on his lap and the nurse stood aside so I could do the honours. Doctor Chang took charge of the scooter thing, and with a double-check that he'd got everything from his room, and after far too many days, we finally walked out of the neuro ward.

As we made our way through the hospital toward the exit, the doc asked us what we had planned for our first day of freedom. "Oh," Justin said with a frown. "I dunno. Probably not much."

"Well, I thought I might get Justin propped up on the couch in front of the flat screen," I said. "There's a Motocross special on Foxtel right now."

He looked back up at me, his grin wide. "Hell yes."

Doctor Chang laughed. "I should have known." Then she stopped at the doors to the outside. "Well, this is as far as I go." We got him out of the chair and onto his scooter, and she looked at us both. "You're gonna do great, Justin. One day at a time. You have all the info, but if you need anything, you can call. And I'll see you in one week for your first appointment."

She waved us off and I slung the overnight bag over my shoulder. "You ready?"

He inhaled deeply and swallowed hard. "Yep." Then he

shrugged his good shoulder. "Well, there's Motocross and iced coffee waiting for me, so yeah."

I laughed, and we made our way toward the car park. It was slow going, and I made sure I walked on his right side so I could catch him should he get dizzy or fall. He didn't though; he just went at his own pace.

But then he did the strangest thing.

We got to the entrance and he saw my blue ute and headed straight for it.

I stopped walking, which made him stop. "What's wrong?" he asked.

"Justin," I whispered. "Which car's mine?"

"The Holden ute," he said, scowling at me like I was an idiot. But then he realised . . . His eyes went wide, his mouth slack. "How did I know that?"

I laughed. "I don't know."

His eyes were comically wide, and he was smiling but stunned and probably confused. "Did you tell me that?"

"Nope."

"Was it in the photos?" he asked.

"I don't think so," I answered. I mean, I couldn't be absolutely certain, but I was pretty sure there weren't any pictures of my ute. "We never talked about it."

"How did I remember that?" he asked, then looked back at the ute. "How did I know you drove a piece of shit Holden when you could have bought a Ford." His eyes darted to mine. His chest was rising and falling hard, and I couldn't help it.

I burst out laughing. "You told me a thousand times that I should've bought a Ford. We joked about it for years."

He opened his mouth and closed it a few times, though he looked a little scared. "I know that. I know that argument. I remember it. Not saying it to you, but just that it was a thing."

I did put my hand to his face this time. I couldn't help it. "You remembered something. Jussy, you remembered something."

His eyes began to swim. "I remembered something."

I had to swallow back my tears. "You did!" I swiped his cheek with my thumb, relishing in the touch for the briefest moment before I pulled my hand away.

"I remembered your car," he whispered. "I just saw it and I knew it, like I'd seen it a thousand times, that it was yours. I mean, I didn't really *remember* it, I just knew it. Like I knew my sister when I saw her. Or how I knew I liked iced coffee."

"But this is better than that," I said. "Because I only bought my ute four years ago. You couldn't have known from before. Not that you knew me when you were in Darwin, but the car is kinda new. You remembered something from within the time you lost, Juss."

He nodded slowly, then put his hand to his forehead. "I did."

I put my hand on his shoulder. "Your head feel okay?"

"Yeah, I think," he said, distractedly. "Headache's still there."

The headaches were a constant. It was only their severity that changed. "Let's get you home."

I helped him into the ute and got his seatbelt sorted, then put his scooter and bag into the back, strapping them in. I got in behind the wheel and buckled up and put the key in the ignition. He had his eyes closed, almost squinting. "You okay?" I asked again. "With being in a car?" I wasn't sure if the accident had affected him on some subconscious level.

He must have been thinking the same thing. "Uh, I think so . . ."

"I'll go slow. If you need me to pull over, just say so. Home is just ten or fifteen minutes away. So it's not too far."

He nodded and I could see he was clearly tired. I turned the radio off to eliminate noise, backed the car out, and slowly made our way home. It was mid-morning, the sun was shining, there was hardly any traffic, but I was hyperaware of every vehicle around us. I had no idea how he'd react if someone pulled into traffic too fast or braked too hard. Thankfully, the trip was incident-free.

I pulled the ute into the driveway and drove around the workshop into the backyard. It was where we sometimes parked to unload groceries and stuff because it was closer to the back stairs. I shut the engine off and gave Justin a smile. "Here we are."

Davo came out of the workshop, wiping his hands, and Sparra followed him into the sunshine. "Here he is!" Davo cried. Davo knew Justin couldn't remember him, but Davo was determined to treat him like he always had.

"They've missed you," I said quietly before getting out. I went around the front of the ute and opened Justin's door, then got his scooter ready, putting it beside the ute. "Okay, getting into the ute wasn't too bad," I said. "Now let's see about getting you out."

He sat side-on, lifting his right leg, and gently lowered it to the ground, but he couldn't quite get leverage with his left arm to help propel himself upward.

"Here," I said, offering my hand. He took it and we slowly got him onto his feet. He smiled with a hint of pain and exhaustion.

Justin looked at Davo and Sparra. "Hey. Um." He made a face as though he was embarrassed. "I'm Justin."

"We know who you are," Davo said, his grin firmly in place. "But I'm Davo, and this is Sparra. It's real good to see you up and about, mate. And this one here—" He pointed his thumb at me. "—hasn't stopped smilin' since there was talk of you comin' home."

"Ugh, thanks, Davo," I said, trying not to blush. "Haven't you got work to do?"

He just laughed, and Sparra added, "Heard him vacuumin' and everything. He hasn't been that nervous since you two first hooked up."

Davo whacked Sparra with the back of his hand. "You're not supposed to talk about that," he whisper-hissed at him.

I sighed. "Seriously, guys."

But Justin chuckled. "Nah, it's okay. Don't sweat it."

I turned to face him. "You wanna hit the couch and watch some Motocross, maybe rest for a bit?"

He nodded. "Yeah." But then he looked at the stairs. "Oh."

"Uh, yeah. Did you want to sit on your scooter for a bit?" I suggested instead.

He shook his head. "Nah. I'm up. If I sit down, I'll be down for a bit. Let's do this."

I handed the scooter and my keys off to Davo. "Can you carry that up for us, please, and hold the door open?"

Davo grabbed it and jogged up the stairs, unlocked and opened the door, and waited.

We got to the bottom of the stairs and he could stand, holding the railing easily enough. If he could use his right arm properly, he'd have no trouble using the railings like crutches, but his arm wasn't up for that. He managed two stairs and looked up to the top as though he was looking up at Everest. "Jesus."

"I have an idea," I said, behind him. "You can say no if you want . . ."

Justin half-turned to eye me. "What?"

"I could put you over my shoulder. It just might make you dizzy, that's all."

"Over your shoulder?" he asked.

"Well, yeah."

"It wouldn't be the first time," Sparra said, then grimaced. "Ah, sorry."

Justin shot Sparra a quick look. "It wouldn't be?"

Sparra gave me an apologetic look, but then he turned back to Justin. "Well, no. It was the State of Origin a few years back, and you backed Queensland and took a shot of Bundy for every try they scored, and anyway, they won by forty points and you were shitfaced. You were gonna sleep down here but Dallas weren't havin' none of that, so he carried you caveman style up the stairs."

Davo laughed. "You spewed upside down all the way up. Funniest shit I ever saw."

I couldn't help but laugh, because that night had been hilarious. But Justin was flagging. His blinks were slow and his words were too. If we left it any longer, he would be taking a nap in the workshop. "What do you reckon?"

"Don't fancy putting my head down, to be honest. Like upside down. Leg pain I can deal with, head pain not so much."

"Yeah, okay, sorry. Good point." I should have known that, but I was glad he spoke up with what he was comfortable with.

"I can do this," he said, more determined this time. He took a deep breath and steadied himself.

I stood behind him, ready to catch him should he fall. "I got you."

He held on to the handrail like crutches, and bearing as little weight as he could on his injured leg, he made one step. Then another, and another. It was slow going, but he was doing this. And so help me, he was determined.

"How's it feel?" I asked, my hands at his waist.

He grunted as he lifted his right leg up to the step he was standing on. "'S okay," he said, panting. "You just wanted to check out my arse, didn't ya?"

Sparra laughed. "There's the Justin we know!"

I laughed at that but kept a hold of him as he made the final step, then helped him onto his scooter. He was breathing hard but he was smiling, clearly pleased with his progress. But he looked exhausted.

I propped his right foot up and helped him push inside. "We're gonna get you to the couch, okay?"

He nodded.

I took his left arm and helped him onto the sofa. I pressed the button that lifted the foot recliner and he settled back with a few rough breaths. He had a line of sweat along his brow. I propped him up with cushions, making him as comfortable as possible.

"How's your head?"

He winced at that and shook his head a little.

I turned to Sparra, who was looking a little uneasy. "Sparra, his black bag in the back of the ute, it's got his meds in it."

He took off and was out the door, but Davo stayed and appeared with a glass of water that he handed to Justin. "You gonna puke, Jusso?" he asked. "I'll get ya a bucket."

Justin shook his head. "Nah. Head hurts though."

I put my hand to his face and let him lean against me a little. "I'm sorry. But you're here now. We'll get you settled in and you can nap in front of the sports channel."

He nodded just as Sparra came back in with the bag. He handed it over, then he and Davo both gave me a nod and slipped out the door.

I got Justin a pain pill and knelt down in front of him. He swallowed the pill without question, a testament to his pain, and let me take the water. "Today was a big day, yeah? But that was the worst of it. It'll get easier every day. Though I reckon me and Davo might work on that motorised seat up the stairs for ya, huh?"

He half-smiled, but his eyes drifted closed and he slept.

I fell back onto my arse and sagged. I knew Justin was exhausted, but I was too. The last four weeks had come down to this. Every mile of hell we'd trudged through came down to Justin finally coming home. And now he was here.

I felt the mountain I'd been trying to move finally budge. We had a long way to go, sure. But he was home. The weight I'd been carrying had lifted a little and its reprieve took the wind out of me.

I was so relieved, so fucking tired, I didn't even have the energy to get up. I simply lay back on the floor in a heap in front of the couch and closed my eyes.

CHAPTER TEN

I WOKE UP WITH A START, wondering where the hell I was and why my neck hurt like a bitch. Was I on the floor?

"Looks like someone's awake," a warm voice said. I turned, my neck protesting loudly, to find Justin still lying on the lounge. But now he had a lump of purring Squish on his chest. Squish had his eyes closed, looking all kinds of contented, and Justin smiled at me. "He certainly knows me."

I sat up, groaning as all the kinks and knots made themselves known. "If I ever fall asleep on the floor again, kick me and tell me to get up."

"You were zonked right out. Figured you must've needed the nap."

I squinted at the clock. Shit. I'd been asleep for two hours. I heaved my sorry self to my feet. "You hungry? I'll make us something."

"Anything that's not hospital food would be great."

I stopped because I had intended to make us a sandwich each, but that was probably the last thing he felt like. "Want pizza? It is your first day out and all. We should have something to celebrate."

"Oh my God, yes." He groaned. "I want the filthiest, greasiest Domino's pizza ever."

I laughed because that was such a Justin thing to say, and gave Squish a pat. He opened his big yellow eyes and gave me a look of proud disdain. "I told you he was coming home," I said, giving the cat a scratch under his chin.

"I woke up like this," Justin said. "He must have found me and decided I looked comfy."

"He's missed you," I murmured. I met Justin's eyes. "I know you don't remember being here, but it's real good to have you back."

He kinda smiled, a bit confused and a bit weirded out by the looks of it, so I changed subjects. "Barbeque Meatlovers, right?"

"Yes, please."

I found my phone and thumbed the app and simply clicked on our last favourited order. My card was already connected; I hit confirm and slid my phone onto the coffee table. "It says thirty minutes."

He squinted at me. "You ordered it already?"

"Yep. They have an app now, on your phone. Makes it super easy."

He frowned. "There's a bunch of shit on my phone I don't know what the hell any of it's for."

I gave him a smile. "We'll get you caught up."

"I sent Becca a text," he said. "Told her I had my phone back. She replied like ten times, so that's something that also hasn't changed."

I snorted at that, then thought of something. "Hey, when you're ready to get up, I can show you around. Bathroom," I said, then the one I'd been dreading . . . "And your bedroom."

He began to sit up, pissing Squish off. "Sorry, little dude," Justin said. "But yeah, the bathroom would be good. I need to pee."

I showed him the button that retracted the recliner and I wheeled his scooter closer. "How's your leg? You gave it a bit of a workout earlier."

"It's okay now," he said, transferring himself to his scooter easily enough. "Those pain pills don't muck around."

He lifted his right foot up onto the footrest and took hold of the handlebar with his left hand. I was certain the pain pill helped immensely, but it was also amazing what a nap did to his energy levels.

"Okay, so you know how I said the unit was kinda basic," I began. "Well, this is the kitchen, dining, and lounge room."

And it was. The unit was basically a large rectangle above a mechanic's shop. One half of the rectangle was the living space, with the kitchen along the end wall and corner, a small dining table, and a three-seater couch facing a big flat-screen TV. The other half of the flat was two bedrooms and a bathroom. That's all there was to it.

I walked to the small hall and he wheeled himself behind me. "Bathroom is here," I said, opening the first door on the left. "It's pretty big. Shower, toilet. Washing machine and dryer are in there too, and the linen cupboard." Then I pointed to the door at the end of the hall. "That's my room," I said, not wanting to dwell on that. So I quickly opened the door opposite the hall. "And your bedroom is here."

He peeked inside at the double bed and nodded slowly. "Gotta use the bathroom first."

"Need some help?" I cringed, but it had to be asked.

"Nah. Be okay."

"Okay, sure. I'll just leave you to it," I said awkwardly, walking back out to the living room. I picked his bag up and slid it onto the couch for him, cleaned the kitchen bench, again, then checked inside the fridge and pantry for what groceries we'd need— anything to keep myself busy.

Finally, I heard the toilet flush and the sink tap turn on and shut off, then a minute or two of silence. I was going to ask if he was okay, but the door opened and he scooted slowly across the hallway until he was staring into "his" bedroom.

The thing was, it was *our* room. It had been our room for five years. But I couldn't expect to sleep in his bed now. We weren't "together" like that anymore. And the very last thing I wanted to do was freak him out or pressure him.

He'd just had his whole world upended. He needed to feel safe here, and if that meant I had to move into the spare room, then so be it. The shitty pull-out sofa bed would be my bed for . . . well, possibly forever.

He wheeled himself into the room, and with a quiet sigh, I left the kitchen and followed him. "This is nice," he said. He was sitting on his scooter just inside the doorway. It was a basic room with a heavy wooden-frame queen-sized bed and a large window that faced the back of the work-shop. The walls were a light grey, doona was dark blue, and there were two bedside tables with old touch lamps I'd had forever. We never needed anything fancy. We weren't the fancy type.

But I'd cleared out my personal things, things like my phone charger and most of my clothes. "Uh, that door is the wardrobe."

He scooted to the left side of the bed—his side—and

touched the bed cover. His eyebrows knitted and he shot me a look.

"What's up? Do you remember something?"

"I dunno," he whispered. "Not a memory. Just something I know."

"What is it?" I asked, my heart in my throat.

"I don't know," he said, a confused and frustrated line between his eyebrows. "It's familiar, but it's not. I don't know how to explain it. Like I know this is my bed, but I can't remember exactly."

"Like how you knew my ute when you saw it."

He nodded. "It's weird. I mean, it's good. I guess. Like knowing what colours are in a painting but not knowing what the picture is. It doesn't make much sense, but it's something."

It made me smile. "It *is* something. And that's two somethings on the first day. That's pretty good."

He was quiet for a long moment. "You said this was my room."

I nodded.

That confused look was back. "Did we . . . We were together? Before the accident?"

I had to clear my throat. "Um, yeah."

"But we didn't share a room . . ."

My mouth was suddenly dry. "I didn't think you . . . Actually, I thought you'd be more comfortable if I took the second room. Some privacy, you know, for when you need space to chill out or just for some alone time, given everything you've been through."

He was frowning at me, and I couldn't bear the weight of his scrutiny.

"We shared a wardrobe," I said. "I mean, the clothes. Shirts, sweaters. After a while we couldn't remember who owned what and we just wore whatever was clean, basically. So if you find something and you want to wear it, go right ahead. Except the Newcastle Knights stuff, that's all yours."

He managed a smile at that. "Who's your team?"

"Bulldogs."

He stared blankly at me.

"Do you not remember them?" I asked because that was well outside of the last five years. The Bulldogs had been around forever.

"Yeah, of course," he said. "I just thought you were a decent guy, and now you tell me you're a Bulldog supporter? I thought I had better taste in men. What the hell happened to me in the last five years."

I laughed because that was such a Justin thing to say. He'd taken the piss out of my footy team since the day he found out. I'd worn an old Bulldogs jersey one day and he'd laughed till he almost cried. He was a Knights supporter to the bone, and we'd ribbed and jibed each other for years.

"Well, your taste in men is just fine," I said with a smile. "Your taste in football teams, not so much."

He chuckled, his eyes bright and happy.

"Dallas?" Davo called out. It sounded like he was at the bottom of the stairs. "Pizza guy's here."

"I'll get it," I told Justin. "Wanna get us something to drink from the fridge?"

He nodded and I went down to collect the pizzas. When I got back, Justin was sliding two cans of lemon soda onto the table, then he scooted back to the kitchen and began opening cupboards. He found plates, and I was going to help him but wanted him to do things on his own. I knew Justin—the old Justin—and I knew if he needed help, he'd ask for it.

He put the plates on the table and scooted back to the cupboards. "Where the hell are the glasses?"

I chuckled. "Cupboard above the sink, to the left."

It meant he'd have to stand up, so I put the pizzas on the table in case I needed to grab him in a hurry. He put his right foot on the ground and stood up, reaching to open the cupboard. He had to duck his head back a bit so it didn't hit him, but he kept his balance and put one glass on the counter, then another, then slowly sat himself back on his scooter. He stacked the glasses and held them in his left hand, then scooted back to the table.

He'd done it. All by himself.

And from the smile he wore, it was easy to see he was pleased with himself.

I forced myself not to smile at him and pointed to the cupboard. "You uh, left the cupboard open."

He snorted. "Don't push your luck."

I laughed and pulled out a seat next to him, then opened the first pizza box. "Your Meatlovers," I said, sliding it closer to him. "And my chicken and pineapple."

He stared at me, wide-eyed. "Okay, what the hell? Chicken and pineapple? How were we together?"

I burst out laughing. "Just shut up and eat yours."

He laughed as well, and for a fleeting moment, it was like nothing was different, like nothing had changed. The way he looked at me, all happy and laughing, made me giddy. It felt a little like the first time all over again.

Like when we'd just got together and everything we did was new. When just a glance from him was enough to make my belly flip. When his smile and his laugh wrapped themselves around my heart.

It was just like that, though somehow maybe, possibly,

even better. I valued it now, like truly knew how much that was worth, and I'd never take it for granted again.

I CARRIED the empty pizza boxes down the stairs to the recycling bin and walked into the workshop. Sparra saw me first. "How is he? You're smiling, so I guess it's all good."

"He's back on the couch watching Motocross, but I reckon he'll already be asleep. He was struggling to keep his eyes open after a belly full of pizza, so I left him to rest. He still needs to sleep a lot."

"How's he settling in?" Davo asked, walking over as he wiped his hands on a rag.

Pretty sure my smile answered for me. "He's good. He remembered my ute this morning, and he remembered the bedroom. Nothing huge, and more just kind of knowing than remembering, but that's pretty damn good. The doc said coming home can trigger stuff."

"That's awesome," Davo said, his grin wide.

"He's still the same, isn't he?" Sparra said. "Like his sense of humour is just the same."

I nodded. "Yeah. He's still the same." All the doctors had warned me about possible personality changes that some people had after a brain injury, but Justin was still the same sweet, funny guy he'd always been—and for that, I was so grateful. "He took the piss out of me for having a Holden and for having pizza with pineapple. And for being a Bulldogs supporter."

They both laughed at that. "Same old Jusso then," Davo said.

"Yep. Anyway," I said. My cheeks were starting to hurt from smiling so much. "Thought I'd tackle that pile of

125

paperwork on my desk. You guys need a hand with anything?"

"Nah," Sparra said. "Not today. I'm just finishing up on the Yamaha; should have it done by this arvo. But we've got the Williams' Kawasakis coming in tomorrow."

Davo nodded. "Four bikes. Drive chain and transmission, brakes. Nothing huge and we can handle it if you need, but if you're gonna be around . . ."

"I'll be here," I said. "You guys have been a godsend. I really appreciate everything. I hope you know that."

Sparra looked like he'd swallowed something sharp; he never was too good at compliments, but Davo gave me a nod. "Any time, mate."

Feeling better than I had in weeks, I went into my office and sat down at my long-abandoned desk. I'd managed to get through some of the urgent stuff over the last month but I was way behind. Knowing Justin was safe asleep upstairs, and with a note by his phone to call me if he needed me, I took a deep breath and started with the top of the pile.

Two hours later my phone beeped with a message. *You here?*

I quickly thumbed out a reply. *Just downstairs. You okay?*

Yeah.

The little text bubble appeared, then disappeared, and then nothing, as though he wanted to say something but stopped himself. I pocketed my phone and ducked out of my office and through the workshop and took the stairs two at a time.

Justin was sitting up on the couch, still a little sleep rumpled. "Hey," I said. "Everything okay?"

He squinted one eye. "Yeah. Just woke up. You weren't here."

I sat on the coffee table in front of him and handed him the note. He read it and frowned. "Sorry. Didn't see it."

"Don't apologise," I said with a smile. "I'm never far away, okay?"

He nodded. "Guess I'm not used to being alone."

I switched from the coffee table to sit right beside him. I took his hand. "Hey. You're not alone. I'll always be around. And during the day, on the rare occasion I ever have to duck out or go run an errand, the boys are downstairs. They'll come straight up."

He looked uncomfortable, embarrassed even, and licked his lips as though his mouth was dry. "They're not you."

I squeezed his hand and fell against the back of the sofa, sitting side-on, looking right at him. The fact he wanted me around made me happier than it probably should have, but his needs were bigger than my ego, and I needed to remind myself of that. "It's been a crazy day, huh? New place, new everything."

He nodded and closed his eyes, clearly still tired. "Took a bit to remember where I was." His fingers tightened on mine. "The only constant thing in my life since I woke up . . . is you."

My heart squeezed to the point of pain. "I'm not going anywhere."

He was quiet for a bit. "Nothing makes sense," he whispered eventually, then opened his eyes to look at me, his dark eyes imploring and so, so familiar.

"What doesn't make sense?"

"I can't remember anything. Like I have everything up to a point, then it's gone. It's just blank. Like I'm trying to remember something that hasn't happened yet."

I squeezed his hand. I didn't know what to say to that but I could at least show him I was listening.

"I can't explain how it feels," he said. "I just woke up and you weren't here and I wasn't sure where I was for a second. Kinda scared me, that's all."

"That's understandable," I whispered. I threaded our fingers and held his hand in both of mine.

"Nothing here is familiar," he mumbled. "But it kinda is. It's hard to explain. I can't remember this place, but it feels right. Like, I feel like I belong here, even though I've never been here before. It's so hard to explain. I'm sorry. I keep talking shit. I just woke up. Guess I'm a bit misty."

"It's okay, Juss. You don't need to apologise. But thank you for telling me how you feel. I'm glad you feel you belong here. This is your place, your things."

He smiled tiredly. "I need to piss. Again."

I snorted out a laugh because apparently this was who we were now. "Okay then, let's get you up."

He groaned. "God, this sucks. Everything's a freaking chore."

I pressed the button on his recliner and the footrest slowly went down and straightened him upright. "It's gotta be a drag for you. Nothing's easy anymore."

He moved cushions out of the way. "Nope."

"It'll get easier every day though," I said, now standing in front of him. I held out my right hand to his left and widened my stance. "Okay, you ready?"

He nodded, took my hand, and I gently pulled him to his feet. He was putting more weight on his right leg but he could only do it for short bursts, but he came to his feet and my hand automatically went to his waist. He was standing up, our bodies so close, our faces so close.

It took my breath away and he chuckled, like he knew exactly the effect he had on me. "Hi," he said gruffly.

I swallowed hard and took a small step back, stepping

out of the trance. "Hi." I pulled his scooter closer and helped him sit on it. "Are you dizzy?" I asked.

When he didn't answer, I looked up from where I was helping his right foot onto the footrest to find him watching me. "Nah. Not dizzy."

"You okay?"

He smirked, that cheeky smile where only one half of his lips curled upward. "Yeah. I'm all good."

"Okay."

He scooted himself into the bathroom, and as soon as he was out of view, I walked to the kitchen and put my hands on my knees and finally sucked in some lungs full of air. God, Jesus freaking Christ. Did he even realise he was flirting? Was he even flirting? Did he remember just what that smile did to me?

No, Dallas. He doesn't remember . . .

The toilet flushed and I stood up straight and got my breathing and stupid heart rate under control.

He scooted out slowly and bypassed the couch and came over to where I was. "Would you mind if I grabbed a bottle of water?"

"You can have anything you want," I replied. I opened the fridge door so he could see inside it. "Anything in the fridge or pantry, or whatever. You don't need to ask." I took a bottle of water out and handed it to him.

"Thanks. Kinda stupid that I need to keep drinking water when taking a piss is a two-man job."

I laughed at that. "Your kidneys will thank you."

"Maybe I could ask the doc to put that catheter back in." He rolled his eyes. "So, you going back downstairs? I mean, to work?"

"It's just paperwork. I can bring it up here if you'd rather have the company."

"No, 's okay." He swallowed and tried to smile. "I'm good now. And you're like two seconds away."

"Sure?"

He nodded. "Sure."

"Okay, well, I better get back to it. I need to get this paperwork done today. They need me on the floor tomorrow and I should get these bills paid. I haven't exactly been around much."

Justin frowned. "Yeah, of course. Sorry. You must . . . be really behind." He turned and backed the scooter up.

"Hey, Jussy," I said gently. He stopped and gave me a sideways glance, so I walked over and stood in front of him. "It was my choice. My priority was you, and I have absolutely zero regrets. I would choose the same again, without hesitation."

He met my eyes. "Still sucks for you though."

I gestured broadly to him. "Not as much as it sucks for you," I said, and he conceded a smile. "No one asked for this. It's not anyone's fault. The universe just handed us a really shitty deal, that's all. And we'll do whatever it takes to get through this. That's what we do. Okay? No guilt, no regrets."

He rolled his eyes. "Are you like some kind of perfect guy? Did they bring out a perfect guy in the last five years that I don't know about?"

That made me smile. "I'm far from perfect. Just you wait till you see how stubborn I can be."

"Like a mule in molasses," he whispered. I stared at him and he gave me a second look. "What?"

"You used to say that," I replied. Whether it was something he used to say before he knew me, from a time when his memory was intact, I couldn't be sure.

"My nan used to say that," he said, but then he shook his head. "Sorry."

"Don't ever apologise."

He searched my eyes for a beat too long, then sighed before he slowly scooted back to the couch. He threw his water bottle on first, then manoeuvred himself onto the sofa, slowly, but by himself, just as Squish came out from the hall. "I wondered where you went," Justin said as he pressed the recline button. Squish jumped on his lap, purring loudly, and they got comfy.

"Can I get either of you something before I go back downstairs?" I asked as I put all the remotes and his phone by his hand.

"Nah, we'll manage, thanks." He gave me a genuine smile. "Thanks. But me and Mr Squish are gonna watch something. Maybe there's a documentary on mice or fish he'd like to watch."

I laughed. "Okay, well, I better leave you to it. I'll just be another few hours, unless I get sick of looking at numbers and decide I should be watching mice or fish with you two."

He was settled in, so I went back downstairs and Davo saw me. "You left in a hurry. Everything okay?"

"Yeah, he's fine. But we could take bets how long it is before he goes batshit crazy with boredom."

Davo laughed, but Sparra obviously overheard. He came over. "My nan had her hip done and we took her jigsaw puzzles and crossword books." He shrugged. "She loved them."

"That's not a bad idea," I thought. His OT had suggested things like that.

"Nah," Davo said. "There's something better than that, and we have a few that need doing too."

"What is it?"

"Puzzles he'd actually be interested in doing. We've got those two old 125 engines that need full rebuilds. All the seals and manifolds need replacing, missing bolts and washers. Cleaning, tuning."

I grinned at him. "That *is* a puzzle he'd like." Those old engines had come off wrecks and had been sat in a corner for years. We were gonna get around to fixing them sometime, just to resell or use on a rebuild. But they needed work and it was time we never made a priority for. "I love that idea. But I might suggest a jigsaw puzzle first. Then when he's sick of doing them and needs to get out of the flat before he goes crazy, we can suggest the engines. His cast comes off next week, so that might be good timing. Give him something new to do, to break the monotony. Because knowing Justin, while he needs the rest and while he gets tired a lot, he's gonna be climbing the walls soon."

CHAPTER ELEVEN

I WAS nervous about Justin's first night at home. He'd got himself changed into some boxers and a T-shirt and brushed his teeth while I cleaned up after dinner. I'd made a chicken salad, after all the crap we'd eaten, and Justin ate it happily, apparently oblivious to my nerves.

The night before he came home from hospital, I'd slept on the sofa bed in the spare room—now my room—because I'd remade his bed with fresh sheets. And while I was excited and grateful to have him home, sleeping in separate rooms wouldn't be easy for me. It was stupid, but it somehow confirmed that things were different between us now.

But giving him a safe place to recuperate was my priority. He certainly didn't need the confusion and pressure of our relationship—a relationship he didn't remember—while recovering from a traumatic brain injury, and I felt like an arse for even thinking about it.

So when he got himself back onto the couch, his leg elevated and his arm supported, he changed the TV channel. "What did you want to watch?"

"I don't mind," I answered, wiping down the sink. "TV shows all suck, but there might be something on Netflix."

He stared at the remote for a while, and when I walked over, he handed it to me. "I dunno how it works," he said, his voice slower and a little slurred. It was always worse when he was tired, especially at night. I took the remote and he gave me a weary smile as he patted the seat right next to him. "Can you sit wi'me?"

"Of course I can."

I sat beside him, not touching, but after a few seconds, he wiggled over and leaned against me, his head on my shoulder. "'S okay?"

"Yeah, of course," I whispered, not trusting my voice for anything more. "You feel okay? How's your head?"

"Mmm, 's okay."

He would have to take his pills before bed, so he couldn't really take anything just yet. We'd organised all his pain meds on an app for his phone and allocated them into those dispensers with each day marked on it, and I'd put the remaining pills in the cupboard above the fridge. We'd marked down all his appointments for the next week on the calendar in the kitchen and in our phones, and during the afternoon he'd written in his journal how he felt about being home and the things he'd 'remembered.' Though as he said, he didn't remember them exactly: my ute and the bedroom. He just knew them. His writing hadn't ever been great, he was certainly never going to win a neat-hand-writing award, but it was a bit worse now.

It was crazy how one huge change was made up of a lot of little changes. There were so many things that were different.

But this, us sitting on the couch together like this, was so very much the same. There was always some part of us touching. The *old us* had always curled up on the couch together. It would seem the *new us* did too.

It wasn't easy because I was trying to separate the two versions of us, to give him the space he needed to heal. This Justin needed to be the one to decide if he wanted an *us*, not me. It didn't help my heart at all when he reached over and took my hand.

I was going to ask if he was okay, but his eyes were closed. He wasn't asleep yet, but he was peaceful, and if he needed to hold my hand to help with that, then I wouldn't ever object.

I told my heart to wait, to be patient, and to give him all the room and support he needed. Because if I was being truthfully honest, I needed it too. Having his head on my shoulder, his hand in mine, helped me heal too.

Would it ever become anything more? Only time would tell.

I had hope though, and my heart clung to that like a lifeline.

After a little while and before he fell asleep, I got his pills for him and a glass of water. He used the bathroom again and scooted into his room. He went to his side of the bed and pulled the covers back, but he was too tired to haul himself up and onto the mattress from his seat so I helped him stand and sit on the edge of the bed. He lifted his leg in carefully and lay down. "Oh yeah. This better than hospital bed," he mumbled, half-coherently.

I pulled the blankets up and resisted the urge to lean down and kiss his forehead. Instead, I swiped my thumb across his forehead and his eyes drifted closed. "Night, Justin. I'm really happy you're home," I whispered.

He hummed something I couldn't understand because he was already asleep. So I watched the rise and fall of his chest for a few seconds until Squish jumped up onto the bed and curled himself in close to Justin's side. "You watch him for me," I said, and Squish replied with a purr.

I left his bedroom door open and the bathroom light on, in case he needed it during the night. But I closed my door because I didn't want him to see that it wasn't really a bedroom. It had a sofa and an old desk with a printer that had stopped working long ago. I crawled onto the sofa bed, the protesting springs loud in the quiet flat.

I hated that I was in here and he was in there, but I was just happy he was home. Day one was done. Doubting I'd get much sleep, and with one ear listening for any sounds from Justin, I closed my eyes anyway, and the next thing I knew it was morning.

I HAD the kettle boiling and was buttering toast when Justin came out of the bathroom. He was squinting his right eye the way he did when his headache was particularly bad. Without a word, I grabbed his pillbox thing and set it on the table and poured a glass of water from the tap. "Here, have this," I said as he scooted over.

He downed the tablets without a word, so I knew it was bad. I put a plate of toast in front of him and he gave me a nod.

I squeezed his shoulder gently. "It'll make you feel better." His shoulder was tight under my fingers. "You're all knots. Want me to massage that out?" I asked as I lightly kneaded his shoulder and neck.

He dropped his head and groaned, his eyes closed. "Ugh, that's good."

"Didn't sleep too well?" I asked.

He shook his head. "No."

"Was something wrong?" I asked, moving my massaging fingers to his right shoulder. I was more careful on this side, but the muscles in his shoulders and neck were painfully tight. "Were you uncomfortable? In pain? Feels like you were tense all night."

"No pain," he answered slowly. His head was still down as he enjoyed the massage, but he obviously wasn't going to elaborate.

"Well, if it's something I can fix, like if you need a heater or a fan, just let me know. Or keeping Squish out; I was worried he'd choose your sore leg to use as a pincushion."

"Nah, he's okay," Justin said quietly. I let go of his shoulder and he hummed. "Feels better already, thank you."

"No worries," I said as nonchalantly as I could. "Want some coffee? Kettle just boiled." I'd bought some decaf for home because that was what we drank now, and it didn't even taste that bad. It was just one more small change we'd had to make.

"Mmm, please." He bit into his toast and I went about making two decaf coffees. It was quiet while he ate, and I made more toast before sitting down at the table next to him. "I had nightmares again," Justin said. "Thought they might have stopped . . ." He finished with a shake of his head.

"Maybe we could ask the doc for something to help you sleep," I suggested. "You can't be waking up with your shoulder that bad. It's not doing your arm any favours." Not to mention how bad the lack of sleep was to someone with a brain injury.

He sipped his coffee. "Hmm. Maybe. I think yesterday took more out of me than I realised."

"It might take a few days to get over it," I said. "You know, getting hit by a truck will do that."

He managed a bit of a smile, and his right eye wasn't squinting now. I assumed his morning meds had kicked in. But he needed a day on the couch, or back in bed even. "I need to shower," he said, frowning. He very clearly hated being so dependent.

I just shrugged like it was no big deal at all. "Then let's get you showered."

The rules were no showering alone. Not that I had to be in there with him, but I needed to be close by should he get dizzy or fall, and the door could be ajar but should never be locked. We put the waterproof cover over his arm and he swore he was fine to get out of his boxers by himself, though that did earn me a smile.

The water started and I stood out in the hall like a fucking pervert. I never peeked; I never even wanted to. I just needed to hear if he was sick and to be close by if he fell. I kept expecting to hear the dull thud of his head hitting the glass shower screen if he did fall.

Of course he was fine. I heard the occasional mumble about something to do with hot water and another one about the smell of shampoo. That one made me smile.

Once I heard the water shut off and him mumble something about the towel, I let out a huge sigh of relief. And happy he wasn't a fall-risk, I left him to it.

I pulled the living room blinds half-closed so it wasn't so bright for him. I put a tray on the couch next to him with a bottle of water, some fruit, and a packet of those soy crisps he liked so much.

He scooted out of the bathroom wearing a pair of shorts and nothing else. "Feel a bit better?" I asked.

He gave a bit of a nod and made his way to the couch.

He manoeuvred himself onto it with some effort today. He really must be feeling ordinary. "Hey, Dallas?"

I turned at my name. It had been so long since I'd heard him say my name ... "Yeah?"

He pressed the recliner button. "Could you get me a blanket or something, please?"

"Yeah, of course," I said. I pulled out an older blanket from the linen cupboard and settled it over him. I made sure the remote controls and his phone were beside him. "I'll just be downstairs. I'm five seconds away, that's all. You call me or text me if you need anything, okay?"

He nodded but he made no attempt to turn the TV on. He simply closed his eyes. "Thank you."

I couldn't help myself this time. I leaned down and kissed the top of his head. "You're welcome."

HE WAS asleep when I checked on him at ten o'clock, though his water was half gone and he'd attempted some grapes and a banana.

The TV was on at lunchtime, the volume low. It was replays of football games from the 80s, something that didn't require much thinking. Certainly no plot to follow and no references to the world in the last five years. Justin was staring at it blankly, but he gave me a smile when I walked in.

"Feeling better?"

"Yeah. A bit. I'm still really tired."

"Then you can take it easy for as long as you need."

He gave a pointed nod to the table. "What's that?"

"Jigsaw puzzles," I replied. "Sparra brought them in this morning. Said they were just collecting dust and thought it might give you something to do when you're feeling up to it. Just for something different to do."

He smiled at that. "Okay."

"You hungry?" I asked. "I was gonna make some toasted sandwiches. Ham, cheese, and mustard. Want one?"

"Sure."

The thing with Justin was that he was always agreeable. Mostly. He was so easy to get along with; nothing was ever an issue. But what I'd noticed with his injuries and how they'd affected him was that he would agree to almost anything. Want me to put on a movie? Sure. Want a sandwich? Yep. Magazine? Okay.

It was as though he had no capacity for thinking, for countering, or questioning. Because if he didn't want a sandwich, it just meant I would follow up with more questions, which would require more thinking. If I'd asked him what he wanted on his sandwich, he'd probably just shrug.

Obviously when he was exhausted, all he could do was just go with the flow.

I sat next to him on the couch and offered him a triangle of sandwich, which he took and ate half of. "What're you working on today?" he asked.

"Some Kawasakis. We have a client who has four of them. He and his three kids all ride, and they're heading off on some camping trip for a few weeks where they ride through bike trails. They get full services done every year."

"Sounds fun."

"Oh, for sure."

He was quiet for a second. "Will I ever ride again?"

Oh, God. My heart hurt for him. "Course you will," I said. "Just need a bit of time first."

He nodded and ate another small bite. "Doesn't feel like it today."

"Do you have any pain?"

He gave a gentle shake of his head. "Nah. Just all misty. And really tired."

"Want to go back to bed? Might sleep easier there."

"Hmm," he said, making a face.

I took that as a no.

"I'll just stay here," he said. "Don't want to sleep all day and not be able to sleep tonight."

"Good point," I said as I finished off my lunch. "Can I get you anything else? Need to use the bathroom?"

He seemed to think for a bit. "I could pee."

"Okay then," I said brightly. "Let's get you up."

I stood in front of him and took his hand, pulling him slowly to his feet. I gave him a second to let his head catch up with the change, and when I went to pull away, he held onto my shirt. He put his forehead on my collarbone. "Stay," he whispered.

I didn't dare move. I didn't dare speak. I even tried not to breathe. But my arm moved without my permission, going around him, slow and measured, and as soon as my palm touched his back, he sighed into me. Then he leaned his face against my chest and settled against me. His body, his warmth.

He was everything.

And I remembered a long-ago conversation. He'd once told me when he was younger and struggling with his sexuality, struggling with finding guys who would treat him right, he never had anyone. And all he ever wished for was someone to hold him and tell him that everything would be okay.

He said it would have saved him years of hurt—trying to fill a void left by his mother who hated that he was gay, and trying to find that salvation in men who all treated him like crap—if he'd only ever been held and told that everything would be okay. He'd told me once it wasn't until he'd met me, after I'd held him and promised him things would be okay, that he believed he was even worth loving . . .

My heart burned for him now.

I held him tighter. "It's okay, Juss. You're gonna be just fine," I whispered. "Everything's gonna be okay."

He breathed in deep, as though he was trying to absorb my words, and let out a shaky breath. He was leaning against me, too tired to hold his own weight, and I held him a little tighter. I rubbed his back, feeling him relax under my touch.

"I got you," I murmured against the side of his head. "It's all gonna be okay, Jussy."

He took a few moments to breathe before he sighed and pulled away. "I really need to pee." He gave me a sad shrug. "But thank you."

"Any time." I put my hand to his face, thumbing just under his eye. "Any time, Justin."

His eyes flickered with something. Was it uncertainty or insecurity? I wasn't sure. It was gone so fast. I pulled my hand away and dragged his scooter over, helping him onto it. He went into the bathroom and I cleaned up after lunch. I replaced his tray with fresh water and fruit and rearranged his cushions for him. I also put his journal beside his seat and the notes from his physio. Not that he *had* to use them, but if he wanted to, he could. He came back out and had obviously splashed water on his face.

"Feeling okay?" I asked.

"Yeah. Better now," he said, managing a bit of a smile.

"Hugs are a pretty strong medicine," I said. "Any time you need one, just ask."

He made a face and chewed on his bottom lip. "We used to do that? Before, I mean?"

I nodded. "Yep. Sometimes you'd have a bad day and I'd hug you until you felt better."

He gave a thoughtful nod. "Seems right. You're good at it, so I guess you had to do it a lot."

I laughed. "Only as required."

He smiled as he transferred himself onto the couch. He seemed happier, and as he pressed the recliner button and his feet slowly came upward, he said, "I don't know whose idea it was to get these push-button recliners, but I'd like to thank them."

"Uh, we actually argued over them."

He shot me a look. "We did?"

I nodded. "You thought it was a waste of money. The ones with the pull handles were cheaper, but I wanted these."

He shook his head, disbelievingly. "I was an idiot. These chairs are great."

I barked out a laugh. "No you weren't. You were cautious with money, that's all."

He pulled his blanket up a bit. "Well, I'm glad you won that argument."

I smiled at the memory of the first night we got that couch. He was still kinda mad about the waste of money, sitting in the same seat he sat in right now, and I'd straddled him on my knees. I pressed the button and we slowly reclined. He'd laughed as I kissed him, and we made out and ended up making passionate love for hours. He never complained about the cost again.

"Me too," I replied. "The day nurse will be here in an hour. Pretty sure it's just a check to see how your first day home went."

"'Kay," he said.

I left him and went back downstairs, and when the nurse arrived, I took her up and introduced them. She asked me about the meds and I showed her everything, but I left them to talk. If he had any concerns, in particular about me, he'd feel more comfortable if I weren't there. But she came back down a short time later, saying everything was fine—his exhaustion was expected after coming home—and that he was resting again.

Me and the boys finished up on the Williams' bikes and had some very happy customers. It was, all in all, a good day. It felt good to be back on the floor, surrounded by familiar sounds and smells of the workshop and to finally be productive at work, but I was glad to call it a day and go check on Justin.

When I walked in, he was sitting on his scooter at the table doing a jigsaw puzzle. "Hey," I said, smiling at his improvement.

"Hey." He frowned at the pieces on the table. "Thought I'd try one of these. But it's not going so well."

I walked over to the table. He'd chosen a beach scene puzzle. "Oh, look at that! You're doing great!" He had all the pieces turned over the right way and he had some colour sorting thing happening and had started to form the border. Putting my hand on his shoulder was such a natural thing for me, to touch him, to show affection, and I pulled away, hoping he wouldn't think too much about it.

When I risked a glance at him, he was blushing a little. His eyes were definitely brighter, so I deduced his headache had lessened. "Thanks."

"I was thinking of having steak and mashed potato for dinner. Maybe some green beans and honeyed carrots. What do you reckon?"

"That sounds really good," he said. "What about . . . what about if I help you with dinner, then maybe you could help me sort out some of these pieces?"

I grinned at him. He was feeling better, and he was sounding more like Justin. "Perfect."

HE SEEMED to enjoy helping me cook, which was nice. It was like old times to me, but it was new for him, and if his smile was anything to go by, he liked it. I think he actually liked being helpful more than the cooking itself, but I'd take his happiness in whatever form it came. I cut up all the steak for both of us so he wouldn't have to attempt it with his clunky cast, and we ate on the couch with the TV off.

He was happier as he ate, affording me small smiles between bites. He liked the nurse, said she was nice, and asked me about the bikes we'd worked on and what we had to do tomorrow. I explained the jobs we had booked in and he listened intently. I asked him if he wanted to venture out tomorrow at all, and he made a face. "Dunno," he replied. "I'll see how I feel. I would like to, but if I need another day of rest . . . I don't want to feel like I did this morning again."

"Fair enough. And I'm really glad you know when to say no. Oh, and your PT is the day after tomorrow, so maybe another day of taking it easy would be good."

"Does she come here or do I go there?" he asked. "She comes here, right?"

"For this one, yes. She comes here. Next week you have two appointments at the hospital though."

He made a face. "That sounds like fun."

I laughed quietly. "Well, getting your cast off will be worth it. And we could get KFC on the way home, or we could swing past the beach if you want or go to the movies? Anything you want to do."

His gaze darted to mine, and his cheeks went pink again. "What, like a date?"

And just like that, my heart rocketed around in my chest. "Uh, sure. If you're up for a date, then yes. I'd like that very much."

He gave me that shy smile he used to wear a lot when we first got together, when he was interested but unsure of putting his heart on the line. "I'd like that too. But dunno what I'll be up for after a long hospital visit."

"That's a week away. You'll be amazed at how much better you feel in a week," I said, trying not to grin too hard. "Anyway, we can have other dates before then that won't knock you around too much. We can watch movies here, do a jigsaw puzzle together. Oh my God," I said, just realising something. "You get to watch *Game of Thrones* for the first time, all over again."

He snorted out a laugh. "Game of what?"

"*Game of Thrones*. A TV show we watched every week, religiously. We have it on Netflix so we can have date night marathons, if you want?"

He smiled, easy and genuine. "I'd like that."

"And we can re-watch every sporting grand final for the last five years. Footy, ice hockey, surfing world championships . . . the list is endless."

"So having the last five years deleted from my mind isn't all bad, right?" he said, trying to smile.

"Well, we need to look for the positives, right? And if doing things again for the first time with you is one of them, then yeah, I'll take it."

He frowned a bit and his eyebrows furrowed. "Did we have a first date?"

"Sure we did. Want me to tell you about it?"

He nodded.

I took his empty plate with mine and slid them onto the coffee table for now. "Well, we had our first kiss in my office, which I told you about."

"Davo locked us in there," he added.

I laughed. "He did. Anyway, so we kissed, and it was incredible. Which kind of sucked because it was the middle of the day and we both had so much work to get done. So yeah, we were a bit handsy, but we needed to cool it and get through to knock-off time. Which we did, by the way. Even though Davo complained the tension was worse by four o'clock." I let out an embarrassed laugh and ignored the heat in my cheeks. "Davo and Sparra left for the day, but you hung around, and I asked you to come upstairs with me."

"Wow, you moved fast," he said with a grin.

"To talk. I asked you upstairs to talk."

He raised a disbelieving eyebrow at me.

"I did, I promise. Actually, as soon as we got through the door, I said, 'Uh, we need to talk,' and you said, 'Well shit, that doesn't sound good,' and you told me later you were worried that I was going to fire you. Which, God, I never would. But anyway, that kinda made the point of the whole need to talk. We needed to put down some professional-slash-personal boundaries and decide how we were going to work this. We both agreed that work was a priority, in the beginning, and we wouldn't let anything else between us become an issue in the workplace."

He nodded. "Sounds fair."

"And we agreed that one-night things weren't our style so we agreed that some actual dates would be fun."

He smiled.

"Then we almost broke my dining table making out on it."

His eyes went wide, his jaw slack. "No . . ."

I laughed. "Yep. Your bodyweight it could hold. Mine on top of yours, not so much."

His grin matched mine. "We did that?"

"Yep. It was old and needed replacing anyway. The legs went on it in the end."

He sighed loudly. "I wish I could remember that."

Me too, Jussy. Me too.

"But that wasn't really a date. I mean, we did eat . . . later that night." I cleared my throat, embarrassed at saying this stuff out loud. "But the next weekend I took you out for dinner. We went to La Mensa, an Italian place, which we went back to a dozen times. I brought you back here afterward, and you kinda never left."

He stared at me. "From one week? I never left?"

I laughed. "Nope. You rented a place when you moved back from Darwin. But it was kinda small and it wasn't great, and you didn't have much because you sold it all so you could move back here. It's cheaper to buy new furniture than it is to pay to move it all a few thousand miles."

"Yeah, true. And what I had in Darwin wasn't worth much anyway," he said. "I can remember Darwin just fine. Like it was just a few weeks ago."

I took his hand. "I know, Jussy. It all must seem strange to have someone explain this all to you."

"It is." He nodded, but his hold on my hand tightened. "But tell me, what happened next?"

"Your lease agreement was coming up on where you were, so you gave notice and moved in here with me. I think we'd been seeing each other for just a few weeks. It was quick and people probably thought we were crazy. But we just . . . clicked."

He leaned his head against the back of the couch but he never took his eyes off me. "I, uh . . ." He shook his head and laughed. "This is so weird. Because I don't know you. I mean, not really. But you know everything about me." Blush coloured his cheeks. "I'd like to, I'd like to get to know you, that is. And I'd really like to go on a date with you."

I laughed, my heart so full it felt like it would burst. I took his hand and squeezed it. "I'd really like that too."

He laughed too, but then he looked right into my eyes and it really felt like he was seeing me for the first time. "But you should know something before we start dating."

My heart skipped several beats. "Oh yeah, what's that?"

"Well, apart from the brain injury and amnesia, which sucks, I also have a broken arm and a leg with a new internal suspension system," he said with a smile, and it made me chuckle. "I'm a bit of a mess, actually. Just so you know what you're getting yourself in for."

I squeezed his hand again, and now that we were 'officially dating' I turned his hand over and kissed his palm, then held his hand to my face. "I know what I'm getting into, Juss. And I can tell you, without any doubt, that you're worth it."

He smiled tiredly at me as he gently scratched my beard. "I like this."

"You've always liked it. I shaved it once and you hated it."

A slow smile caught his lips and he slow blinked. "Sounds about right."

"You're tired," I whispered. "Why don't you go get ready for bed and I'll tidy up in here."

He sighed. "Hate not being able to do stuff."

"I know. But it'll get better. I know it seems slow to you, but I see improvements every day."

"Today sucked."

"Well, today sucked because yesterday we did too much. We know now that reaching your limit isn't worth it. But I reckon tomorrow you'll be as good as gold."

"Hope so. Got a date with a real hottie tomorrow night."

I laughed. "Is that right?"

"Yep."

"That's a coincidence," I said, smiling. "Because I do too."

He looked at me, his brow creased, his face sad. "You do? But . . ."

I laughed and rubbed his arm. He was obviously too tired to process sarcasm, another change since his accident. "My date is with you, Juss. You're the cutie I have a date with."

"Oh." He shook his head and laughed. "Sorry. Tired."

"Come on," I said, standing up. I held out my hand and pulled him to his feet. We were barely an inch apart and he put his forehead on my chest again and sighed.

"You do good hugs," he mumbled.

So I wrapped my arms around him again, holding him tight and breathing him in. He was heavy against me and I rubbed his back. He let out another sigh, long and loud, and then he got heavier. "Okay," I said, waking him up. "You need some sleep."

"Jigsaw puzzle," he mumbled.

"We can do that tomorrow."

I helped him onto his scooter and he sighed again, his eyes heavy-lidded, but he got himself to the bathroom. I took our plates back to the sink and had the washing up almost done by the time he came back out. He took his night pills and I helped him into his bed. He was using his leg more, but with only one arm and being so bone-tired, it was all too much.

Squish joined him as soon as I had the covers pulled up and I left the two of them sleeping. I finished cleaning up and put everything away, and I never stopped smiling.

He wanted to date me. He wanted to go on actual dates, and he wanted to know more about me. He liked holding my hand and he liked my beard. He blushed like he used to when we first met, when we were first together, and he was nervously excited about being with me.

And that gave me butterflies.

Actual tummy jitters. I was so happy, I went to bed excited for what tomorrow might bring.

BUT THEN, somewhere in the dead of night, a scream woke me up. I shot bolt upright in bed, wondering if I'd dreamed it . . . But then a gasp and sob echoed from the room across the hall.

"Dallas? Dallas, please."

CHAPTER TWELVE

I FLEW OUT of bed and into Justin's room. He was sitting up on the bed with his left hand on his head, and he was breathing hard. "Hey," I whispered.

He looked up at me. His eyes were wide, even in the dark room. He shook his head. "Dream."

"Oh, baby," I said, going to him. I sat on the edge of the bed next to him and put my hand on his arm. "You're okay."

He sobbed and sniffled. "Stay. Please?"

"Of course," I said. I went around to my side—or rather, what had been my side—and slipped in under the covers. I slid over and urged him to lie back down and gently pulled him into my arms. He came willingly, snuggling into me just like he used to do. His head was on my shoulder, and his plastered arm was heavy on my chest but it felt good. The weight of it was comforting. I rubbed his back and whispered sweet nothings into the top of his head.

Justin's ragged breathing evened out, and in no time at all, he was out like a light.

He slept soundly, like he hadn't slept that good in weeks. It was a deep, heavy sleep, and I smiled at the ceiling. I knew that this meant different things to us. It was purely to comfort him, but God, it was a comfort to me too.

Our breathing synced, the rise and fall of our chests, our heartbeats . . . I closed my eyes, relishing in this most wonderful feeling.

The next thing I knew, it was morning.

I WAS up before him and thought it would be best if he didn't wake up and freak out that I was in his bed. I slipped out from under the covers and pulled on a shirt, then went and made us some breakfast. I carried the tray of decaf coffee and toast into the room and he stirred awake.

"Morning," I said, unable to keep from smiling.

"Mmm," he said, trying to wake up.

"Breakfast in bed today," I said.

He sat up, leaning against the headboard, bleary-eyed. "Oh, morning."

"How do you feel?"

"Good." He looked to my sleep-rumpled side of the bed. "Oh. Sorry about last night."

I slid the tray onto the bed. "Don't apologise. It was fine. I, um, actually, I slept like the dead."

He hummed. "Me too. I slept all night. Apart from the nightmare . . . but when you were here, it was . . . good. Best sleep ever."

I handed him a coffee. "Do you remember the nightmare?"

He shook his head. "Nah. It's just darkness and falling. It's awful." He sipped the coffee and sighed. "But I dreamed the other dream again, I think. Afterwards. I dunno. Not much makes sense in my head. It's hard to tell if it's a dream or reality. If I'm remembering something or if it's just a dream."

The other dream? "What was it?"

He made a face. "The poster dream."

Oh, that's right. The Harley Davidson poster.

"I dunno. It's like a sign or a poster, I think. Whether it's just a dream or if I saw it one time, I dunno."

I chuckled and bit into a piece of toast. "Dream of bikes often?"

He laughed quietly and put his cup down and picked up a slice of toast. "Not really. This Harley poster is a repeat though."

"You've dreamed of it often?"

He nodded as he chewed and swallowed. "I thought there might be something like it here. It feels like it should be at home. Is there a poster in the workshop?"

"Nope. There's a KTM poster, which you put up. And a Yamaha one the rep gave us to match your KTM one as a joke. And just some bike calendars and promo posters for tyres and stuff. But no Harleys. We've been to a few trade shows though. Maybe you saw something there. The doc said what comes back to you could be random."

He shrugged it off. "Something not random would be good." He washed the last of his toast down with a sip of coffee. "God, I wish I could cut this cast off. It's itchy as hell. I'm just about done with it. Do we have any saws downstairs? Angle grinders?"

"You're not using an angle grinder on your arm."

"A hacksaw?"

"I'm going to go with a hard no on that one too. I'll drive you to hospital and you can beg them to take it off before you try to use power tools."

"Today?"

Shit. He was being serious.

"If you want."

He took another mouthful of coffee and seemed to consider his options. "Do you think they'll take it off for me?"

"I think they will if I tell them you want to use an angle grinder on it."

He smirked, then it faded. "Shit. I have the nurse and physio coming today."

"We can ask them if you're ready to have it taken off. If they say yes, then we can go tomorrow."

He sighed. "I just want my body back, ya know? I don't want the cast or the scooter thing anymore. I can deal with the amnesia—well, I can't but I don't have much choice—but if I could just walk to the freaking bathroom, that'd be great."

"It's frustrating," I said.

"Beyond that."

"Well, hopefully the doc will say yes to taking the cast off. The last X-ray was good and you've had no pain."

He eventually smiled. "You always know what to say."

"No I don't," I admitted. "Not always."

"I think you do. Like just now when you said you'll make more coffee and toast while I go pee. That'd be great, thanks."

I laughed at that. "Message received and understood." I took the tray from the bed and went back to the kitchen to start on more coffee and toast while he got himself to the bathroom. When he came back out, he used his scooter, of course, but he was using his right leg more and more, which was a good sign. His eyes were bright and he was happy.

A complete one-eighty from the day before. It was amazing what decent sleep could do.

He took his pills, ate the toast, and took a long sip of coffee. "What time are my appointments again?"

"Physio at nine, nurse at ten." It was just seven-thirty now.

"So, I have enough time to come downstairs for a bit first?"

"Oh, sure. Do you think you're up for it?"

"Yep."

"You don't think it might be pushing your luck after how tired you were yesterday?"

"Nah. I feel really good today. Probably best I've felt since I woke up. From the accident, I mean. Not woke up this morning."

I snorted. "Yeah, I gathered that."

"And anyway," he added, "if I get too tired, you can carry me back up the stairs."

"Is that right?"

"Yep."

He was in such a good mood, I didn't want to dampen it with my worrying. "Then I better go get showered and get ready for work."

When I walked back out, dressed for the day, I saw he was dressed too but he'd also washed up our few breakfast things. "You didn't have to do that," I said, nodding to the sink.

"I want to. I need to do my share. What I can do, at least."

"Well, thank you. I appreciate it."

He beamed, then took a steadying breath. "Okay. I want to see the workshop and some sunshine, and I have about an hour before my first torture appointment."

I went to the front door and held it open. "Then let's do this."

He stood at the top of the stairs, holding onto the railing while I took his scooter down to the bottom, then I went back up to the second step from the top. "Right. One step at a time."

He did the first few steps, slow and somewhat awkwardly. "Ugh. Going up's so much easier."

"It's okay. We got this," I said, keeping my hands on him. He took another step, then another and another, and finally he was at the bottom.

His grin of accomplishment was beautiful.

He got back on his scooter and put his right foot up on the footrest, and I unlocked the huge roller door and lifted it up. This place had once been a regular mechanics so the roller doors were wide and tall enough to let a truck through. I went inside, flipped the lights on, and unlocked the matching roller door at the front of the shop. I unlocked the padlock on the front gates and opened them wide, and when I went back inside, Justin was sitting on his scooter in the middle of the workshop.

He had his eyes closed and his serene smile damn near took my breath away.

"I know this smell," he said.

Every mechanic's shop smelled of grease and oil, tyres and exhaust. It permeated every surface. "Smells like work to me."

He chuckled but shook his head. "No. I know this smell, Dallas." He swallowed hard and looked down toward the office. "And I know that's my station. And I know there's a fridge in the breakroom with a scratch down the door. And I know there's an old radio on the bench in the corner and it gets better reception when it rains . . ." He put his hand to his mouth. "Oh my God, I remember."

He remembers . . .

He shot me a look, his eyes wide and a little watery. "I remember this."

I went to him and cupped his face in my hands. "You remember it." My voice was a whisper. "Baby, you remember."

"I remember."

I had to stop myself from kissing him. I wanted to, God, how I wanted to. I was just so happy I could have cried! I dropped my hands and looked around the workshop, trying to see it through his eyes. "What else do you remember?"

"I don't know. Nothing really. Just bits and pieces. And it's not really a memory. It's just that I *know* where my station is. I *know* about the fridge and the radio. I just know."

"That is so awesome," I said, because it really was. All these tiny pieces of the puzzle would eventually help form the picture of his missing years. The fact I wasn't yet any of the pieces stung a little, I couldn't lie.

He remembered this place. He remembered my ute. He remembered tiny pieces of our lives.

But he didn't remember me.

Justin scooted down to the office, peeking in, then he looked in the break room. He grinned when he saw the fridge with the scratch. "How did it get scratched like that?"

So he remembered the fridge and the scratch, but he didn't remember being with me when we bought it.

"Bought it like that. It was one of those clearance sales of damaged stock. They couldn't sell it at full price, but there's nothing wrong with it. Apart from the scratch."

He scooted back slowly, looking at the different work stations: his, Davo's and Sparra's. Being down here obviously made him happy. Eventually his eyes went to our bikes, and more importantly, to his. His wide gaze shot to mine, and he grinned. "Is that mine?"

"Sure is."

He scooted over to it and touched the tank, the seat. "Holy shit."

"You'll ride again," I said. "One day."

He nodded. "One day." Then he looked around, searching for something. "There's no poster of a Harley."

"What?"

"The Harley Davidson poster I see in my dreams. It's not here. I know you said it wasn't, but I thought there might be something . . . It just feels so familiar, like it's something I see all the time."

Before I could question him on that, Davo drove into the yard. He and Sparra got out, bickering about something on the radio as they walked in. "Heyyyy," Davo said as soon as he saw Justin. "Look who finally decided to turn up for work." He offered him a left-handed bro-shake, and Justin laughed as he took it.

"Sorry, had some time off," Justin said. "Apparently. Like five years or something."

We all laughed, and Sparra shook Justin's hand too. "Good to see ya up and about, mate."

"Yeah, feels good," he said, still smiling. "Hey, have either of you guys got an angle grinder or an electric saw?"

I snorted. "Juss, you can't cut your cast off with a power tool."

Davo laughed. "Well, we *could*." Then he sized up Justin's arm cast. "Just how fond of the arm are you?"

I snorted. "Exactly my point."

Justin laughed, but then he tapped the cast with his knuckle. "It's driving me crazy. My arm is so freaking itchy."

"My brother used to shove Mum's knitting needles

down his to scratch his arm," Sparra said. "We don't got no knitting needles, but I reckon a welding rod might work."

Davo brightened. "Or what about a long reach screwdriver? They're heaps long and skinny."

I shook my head but couldn't help but laugh. I guessed this was what happens when a group of mechanics tries to find solutions for an itchy arm stuck in a cast. It made me happy as the three of them went off in search of something resembling a knitting needle for Justin to scratch with under his cast. They weren't just workmates, but they were his actual mates, and he needed them.

All the pieces of the puzzle, Dallas. Not just the pieces of you.

Turns out the long reach screwdriver was a bit bulkier than they'd first thought, and the welding rod was a no-go as well.

"Here," I said, holding up a pro-lock tool. "Try this."

Sparra laughed. "Ah, when in doubt, use the slim jim."

Justin grinned as he scooted over to me. "Break into cars often?"

"Not since I was a good-for-nothin' teenager, no," I admitted. "Now I keep it in case someone locks their keys or their kid in a car."

He shoved it down the top of the arm cast and groaned. "Holy shit, that feels so good."

"We have a winner!" Sparra cried.

But I was still stuck on Justin's groan and the look of bliss on his face. God help me . . .

Davo nudged me with his elbow. Bastard never missed much. "Work to do," Davo said as he walked off, still smirking.

Right, yes. Work.

Davo called out, "Jusso, you're with me."

I opened my mouth to object, but Justin gave me a grin before he scooted off after Davo. Sparra clapped my back. "You snooze, you lose," he said with a shit-eating grin. "You get to help me. I got that seized-up Honda to pull apart."

So for the next little while, I helped Sparra with that while keeping one eye on Justin. Davo had him holding some boxes. I heard Davo say, "You're not useless. You still got one good arm," as he piled on another box. I might have objected, but Justin's smile told me to shut my trap.

"He's better today," Sparra said quietly.

"Yeah. He got some decent sleep. Makes a helluva difference." I looked over to Justin and Davo, who were now both in front of a bike Davo was working on. It was an old Yamaha in for an overhaul, and Davo was talking about something to do with the front forks. "He remembered a few more things," I said to Sparra. "Just little things, but it's something, at least."

"Oh man, that's awesome!" he said, his enthusiasm trailing off. "That's a good thing, right?"

I shook my head in some attempt to clear the self-centred funk. "Yeah, it is. It's great."

"But?"

"But nothing."

"But it weren't about you," he whispered, more insightful than I'd have given him credit for.

"It weren't about me," I said, just as quietly. "Which shouldn't matter."

Sparra just kept right on working, trying to get a spark plug out. "Dallas, he's been over there with Davo for three minutes and he looked back over here for you about ten times already." His gaze went from the spark plugs over to Justin and back again. "Make that eleven. He's still yours. No memory loss gonna change that. I never did see what he gone fell in love with you once for, and now he's about to do it twice."

I laughed at that, but Sparra's words—as blunt as he was —really hit me hard. I kept my back to Justin and Davo. "Has he been looking over here?"

Sparra shook his head and cranked the handle of the spanner, straining to get it to budge. "Does Davo need to lock you both in the office again?"

I snorted. "Ah, no. Probably not."

Just then, a car pulled into the yard and Justin's physiotherapist got out. "Jusso, you're up."

He scooted over to the open doorway. "Oh good. My dial-a-torturer is here."

She laughed at that but gestured to him, up and down. "But look at you. Shouldn't you be taking it easy?"

"I'm not working or anything," he said. "And I've only been down here for about thirty minutes."

She rolled her eyes like she'd heard it all before. "So, we upstairs?"

"Yep. This way," he said, leading her through the workshop to the back stairs. I followed them, of course, because he was going to need me on the stairs. He stood up at the bottom, holding onto the railing, and I carried his scooter up before darting back down to help. He managed the stairs well though; going up was much easier than down. And his PT watched on like it was a test, which it probably was.

But he got to the top without too much effort—a vast difference since his first day—and he scooted inside. He didn't need me to stay so I left them to it, and she was already asking him a whole bunch of questions by the time I got out of earshot.

We had a delivery truck arrive with boxes of parts, and I figured it was a good time to run through a quick stock count. A short while later, I heard a female voice ask where I was, and Davo appeared with Justin's PT in tow. I put my clipboard down. "Oh, you're done already?"

"Yeah, he's had enough of me for today."

"Is he okay?"

She laughed. "He's doing great. He managed the stairs perfectly. Which I told him I wasn't too happy about but made him promise that he'd never attempt them, up or down, by himself."

"Yep. I told him that too. Did he tell you that his coming-home day wrecked him? He was so tired yesterday. He only kinda come good yesterday afternoon, but he's been great this morning."

"Yeah, he said that. I told him he should rest all afternoon. He said he would try." She rolled her eyes at that. "But he's been doing his exercises, which is good, and the jigsaw puzzle was a good idea. I've given him new exercises, and if he gets the cast off tomorrow— and that's a big if— he'll need to work on that arm."

"He asked about getting his cast off?"

"Oh yes."

"Did he tell you about the angle grinder?"

"The *what*?"

I snorted. "He wanted to take it off with an angle grinder, but I said no."

"Well, thank God for you," she said with her hand to her heart. "Keep him away from power tools, and I'll see you both next week. You keep looking after him and he'll be right as rain in no time at all."

Smiling at that, I waved her off and I wanted to go check on him but didn't even get to the bottom of the stairs before another car pulled in. It was his nurse, so I showed her upstairs too. Justin was getting a bottle of water out of the fridge when we came in. After seeing he was fine, I headed back to the door, but Justin called out, "Dallas? Can you stay?"

"Sure," I said, not really knowing why he wanted me to stay. But when I sat beside him, he was quick to take my hand. "You okay?" I asked.

He nodded but glanced toward the nurse, who was still getting out her equipment. She checked his meds and his journal, took his blood pressure, his temperature, shone her little light thing in his eyes and ears. She sat on the coffee table and asked him a whole bunch of questions about how he was handling being home, all while writing everything down.

She checked the movement of his fingers on his plastered hand, checked over his injured leg, and was happy with how everything was progressing, physically. He was exactly where they expected him to be, if not a little further ahead.

"Headache?" she asked.

"Yeah, it never really goes away. Just get used to it, I guess. I don't like taking the pills, but I can tell when they're wearing off."

"Any nausea with the headaches?"

Justin shook his head. "No."

"Good." She smiled. "And in your journal, you said you've had some memory triggers?"

"Well, yeah. More today, just this morning, so I didn't write them in yet. But it's hard to explain. It's not like a memory with anything attached to it." He licked his lips and squeezed my hand, and I knew this was what he needed me here for. "It's just things I know that I know. Like I knew Dallas' ute when I saw it. I knew it was his. But there were no flashback scenes of us driving anywhere, or being in the ute at all. I just knew it was his. And I knew the fridge in the break room had a scratch down the front. I didn't see it, I knew before I looked in there. But there was no memory of it, I just knew it was there."

"Okay, that all sounds perfectly normal," she said gently. "I'm not a neurologist but I work with a lot of traumatic brain injuries, and what happens for one person will differ to the next. You should definitely speak to your doctor though."

"So why is it stuff that doesn't matter?" he asked. "I never cared about the fridge before. I never cared about the stupid old radio, but I knew it was in the corner, and I knew it got crap reception unless it was raining outside." He shook his head. "Why do I remember useless shit like that?"

"Some people say that the beginning of regaining memories is like poking pinholes in a dark fabric, letting tiny circles of light in. Little ones at first, and there's no saying what comes through the holes. Sometimes it seems irrelevant, like you said, but you are recovering some memories. Some people don't even get that."

He sighed. "I know. I just . . . I guess I hoped . . ." He looked at me, frustrated and sad.

"I think he wants to know why he can't remember me?" I offered gently.

Justin's face crumpled. "It's all I want. Just something. I don't care about the goddamn fridge. I want memories of you," he said, his expression so vulnerable. "And I want to feel what goes with it. That's the hardest part. It's not just losing the memories. I lost the feelings as well, and I want that back."

"Oh, Juss," I said, putting my hand to his face. "We'll get back to that. You fell in love with me once, what's to say you can't love me twice?"

His eyes welled with tears. "God, that is so unfair to you. I hate how unfair it is to you. Every time I say or do something that makes you think I've remembered more, you get a look in your eyes, like hope. And to see it fade out when you realise I still don't remember you, it just fucking kills me. It's like a light going out, every time. I wish I could remember. I want to, so much. God, you have no idea." He was mad, about as pissed off as I'd seen him. I wanted to reassure him, but he needed to vent and get this out. He deserved that.

"And you know what?" he said. "It's unfair to me too. I hate that it was taken away from me. Not just my memories, but who I am. Who I was. Who *we* were, Dallas. I want memories that mean something. I want memories that I can feel. Instead, all I get is a nightmare where everything's black and I'm falling and that scares the shit outta me, or some weird Harley Davidson poster that I need to find. I can't explain why, but it's important."

"I'm sorry," the nurse said. "A poster?"

Justin nodded. "It's so stupid. But I see this poster and I feel it in my chest. Like right here." He put his hand to his heart. "Like it means something to me I can't explain. It means the world to me and I can't even describe it, but I can feel it."

"Try describing it," I said. "Tell us what you see. Maybe we've seen it somewhere."

He wiped at his eye and shook his head. "It's a Harley Davidson poster, or at least I think it is. The poster with the logo, but in my dream there's no words. Nothing in my brain makes sense. The tighter I try to hold it, the more it disappears."

I squeezed his hand. "Oh, baby."

The nurse was scrolling on her phone. She turned the screen toward us. "Like one of these?"

He scanned the pictures of different Harley Davidson posters, shaking his head. "No . . . no . . . no." Then he froze. "That one. With the wings."

She tapped on it and made it bigger. "This one?"

He nodded quickly. "That one. With the wings. What does it mean?"

I looked at the picture, then looked at Justin, and . . . holy shit. It felt as though the world had stopped turning. I laughed and then had to bury my face in my hands so he didn't see me cry.

"Dallas, what is it? What's wrong?" Justin asked. "You know what this means?"

I dropped my hands, not caring if I fucking cried in front of them. I simply didn't care. I began unbuttoning my shirt to some very strange looks from both the nurse and Justin, but I pulled my shirt off, then pulled my T-shirt over my head so they could see my chest.

Or, more importantly, the two huge wings tattooed across my chest.

Justin stared at the tattoos, then his wide eyes met mine. "It's you. Oh my God, it's you." He burst into tears and put his hand to his mouth. "I remember you. My heart, all this time, oh God . . ."

I pulled him in for a hug and he cried against my chest for a second until he pulled away and pushed my arm. "You didn't tell me you had this tattoo!"

"I wasn't about to be half-naked in front of you. And you told me your dream was of a Harley Davidson poster!"

"I said it didn't make sense. Don't blame me, my brain got scrambled, remember?"

I burst out laughing, so relieved. So very relieved.

He remembered something about me.

I put my hand to his face, so desperate to kiss him. To feel his familiar lips, his mouth, to hold him, kiss him, taste him . . .

Until the nurse cleared her throat.

"Oh," I said, pulling my hand away. I swallowed hard and shook my head. I had to wipe tears from my face. "Sorry."

"Don't apologise," she said, smiling. "If only every home visit was like this." She got to her feet and started to pack up. She told us to keep doing everything we were doing, to keep writing down in the journal every day, and to call if anything changed.

Just as she got to the door, I remembered something and followed her. "Uh, sorry. The cast. It's due to come off next week. Can he have it off sooner? Please? Like tomorrow?"

She gave Justin a stern look. "If he promises to wear the collar and cuff."

I baulked. "The what?"

"Collar and cuff. It's a sling to support the upper arm bone from the shoulder down."

"Oh." I made a face, because boy, collars and cuffs had a completely different meaning. "Thank God, I thought you meant—"

She raised her hand. "I know what you meant." She gave us a wink, told Justin to rest well, and promised to see us next week. Then she was gone.

I closed the door, and when I turned to face Justin, he was standing up. He took some very tentative steps toward me without the scooter, without any assistance. He was slow and trod gingerly on his sore leg, but he was determined.

He came to stand in front of me. I held his good arm,

taking some of his weight. He trailed his fingers across my tattoo with the barest of touches. It sent a shiver through me. "I remember," he whispered. "Not you, exactly. But I remember something. I remember these tattoos. And I remember how you made me feel. And I don't know you the same as you know me, but my heart does. This is the only memory I can feel." He looked at me with tears in his eyes. "My heart remembers you."

I ran my thumb along his cheek and gently lifted his chin and oh so slowly pressed my lips to his. His lips were soft and warm, his taste familiar. He closed his eyes and leaned into me, letting himself be held. And even though we'd kissed thousands of times, this was our first.

Our very first kiss all over again.

CHAPTER THIRTEEN

JUSTIN

FINALLY SOMETHING MADE SENSE.

Finally.

When I first woke up in that hospital, everything hurt. Every part of me. Even with the drugs, my brain still registered pain. It was muted and simmering, but it pulsed under the surface. Pain like you cannot imagine.

My leg, my arm, my chest, but my head.

Wow.

The pain in my head. It was bewildering.

I don't remember the first few days. It all passed in a blur of excruciating pain and nausea, dizziness, vertigo, beeping machines and the cold, metallic hum of drugs.

Then things came back to me in ebbs and flows. The doctors, the nurses, that warm, strong hold on my hand that kept me tethered to reality.

I knew who I was. My name was Justin Keith, I was born in Newcastle, New South Wales, but now lived in Darwin, Northern Territory. I was twenty-five years old.

Except I wasn't.

Apparently.

At first I thought they were joking. Until the doctors became serious and started running more tests and they brought me newspapers that showed the date five years into the future, which was a pretty cool trick.

Except it wasn't.

Apparently.

And all the while, there was that guy who I saw all the time. He was sexy as hell, had brown hair with a tint of grey at his temples. He had dark circles under his blue-grey eyes, and there was a bleakness to him that told me this was all real.

I was thirty now, apparently.

I'd moved back to Newcastle almost five years ago and I worked as a mechanic. That made sense because I *was* a mechanic, and I hadn't been having the best time in Darwin, so that wasn't so hard to believe.

But how the hell was I thirty?

How did five years just disappear?

It felt like someone had written my life on a whiteboard, then wiped the last five years off. I had zero recollection. Zero knowledge, zero connection.

And that was the hardest part. The emotional disconnect. I had no emotional attachments to anything or anyone that had been part of my life in the past five years. I couldn't remember them, like they'd never existed. How could I feel something for someone who never existed?

They told me that handsome stranger was my boyfriend, which might have been the craziest part of the whole nightmare, because how the hell could someone like me jag someone like him? But no, not even just boyfriend, but live-in boyfriend. Oh, and he's my boss too.

I didn't know him, not the first thing about him, but I could see how sad he was and how hopeful he'd get, or a hint of light in his eyes before it faded away when reality dawned.

No, I didn't know him.

But I liked him, and I trusted him. I couldn't explain why, I just did.

Could this have been some Jason-Bourne-type plot to play evil mind games with me? Well, it was highly unlikely. But no. Not Dallas.

He was big and burly, but he was gentle and kind. His smile made my days in hospital bearable. My days were filled with tests and physio, pain and more pain. My nights were filled with strange dreams, which at first were heavily medicated, but as the doses decreased, the weirdness increased.

The falling nightmare was dark and awful, filled with fear and the unknown. My therapist said it sounded like symbolism for the accident and not knowing what the future might bring. I wasn't convinced. It was just fucking falling and darkness to me. And it was a fresh hell every time. You'd think you'd get used to it, but no.

My other dream was different. It was a pair of wings. But it was misty, like my mind, though it wasn't swirling around the wings. It was covering them, as though my mind wasn't ready to show me the whole picture. I was certain they were the wings from the Harley Davidson vintage ads I'd loved as a kid. At least, that's what they reminded me off. That was all I had to go by.

But it was how they made me feel . . . that was the strangest part. Just like the falling dream was fear and a screaming heart rate, the wing dream was comfort and safety. It was love. Which made no sense.

My therapist jumped straight onto the wings-equal-religion train, and how the warmth and safety I felt might have been me wanting to reach out to God. I told him I had amnesia, not delusions. It wasn't symbolic of heaven or angels . . . I knew that.

"There must have been a poster at my home or work," I'd said, and it was plausible enough.

But there were no such posters in the flat or at work.

Because Dallas had them tattooed on his fucking chest. And my beacon to him, my warmth and safety, had been right in front of me the whole time.

I wasn't kidding when I said I wanted to know him, to date him. I wanted it more than anything. Me coming home from the hospital had proven that. He'd been amazing. He gave me independence when I needed it, and he helped me when I needed it. He was considerate and kind and funny, and he smelled so good . . .

And he was my Harley Davidson poster. He was my wings dream, what my heart yearned for. What my heart was trying to show me.

And all those weeks wondering why I couldn't remember him or what he meant to me were over. Because now I knew.

I walked over to him, limping and slow, but so help me God, I was going to do this on my own. I stood in front of him and traced my fingers over the wings I'd seen in my dreams. *I knew these tattoos.* I looked up into his blue-grey eyes, and my heart . . . my heart knew.

"I remember," I whispered. "Not you, exactly. But I remember something. I remember these tattoos. And I remember how you made me feel. And I don't know you the same as you know me, but my heart does. This is the only memory I can feel." I took in his handsome face. "My heart remembers you."

My heart remembers you.

He took my face in his hands and kissed me, tender and sweet, but with emotion he could barely contain. When he broke the kiss, he pressed his forehead to mine, his eyes closed. "Oh, Justin," he breathed. "My heart remembers too."

"You're a really good kisser," I whispered. I was giddy and excited and so fucking relieved. It made him laugh.

He thumbed my cheek and scanned my face, settling on my eyes. "That's not the first time you've said that to me."

"I'd like to do more of it, if that's okay?"

He grinned. "That's very okay."

But as he brought his lips to mine once more, I stopped him. "Uh, wait."

"What's wrong?" His expression quickly worried. "Is it your leg? Headache?"

"No." I took his hand and laced our fingers, unable to stop my smile. "I know this is going to sound weird, considering we live together and considering what I assume we've done . . . in the bedroom." God, that was awkward to say out loud. "But I'd like . . . I'd, uh . . ." I sighed. How could I ask this of him? When he'd already given up so much? "My entire life got thrown upside down. Everything I thought I knew is different now, and . . ."

One corner of his mouth curled upward. "You want to get to know me first."

My cheeks flamed. "Am I that obvious?"

"Obvious, no. But I know you, Juss. And when we first got together, you wanted to know me first."

"I thought you said I moved in with you just weeks after we first kissed."

"You did." He laughed. "And it was an intense few weeks. But you said you'd had enough of shitty men and one-night stands."

I nodded. "Those I remember." Hurt flashed in his eyes. Because I remembered them and not him. "Sorry, Dallas. I know that's not fair on you."

He shook his head. "Don't apologise. It's not your fault. There are pieces of you that are a part of me, and I'll help you find them. I promise you, Justin. I don't care how long it takes. I'll wait until you're certain. I'll wait forever if I have to."

"I don't think it'll take forever," I said, marvelling at the square angle of his jaw, the warmth in his eyes. "Our first date tonight will be a good start."

His grin widened and he let out a laugh. "That sounds good to me."

"You don't mind? I mean, we live together and I'm guessing we've gone further than kissing before. I mean, I still have that photo of me and we're very clearly doing a lot more than kissing in that photo."

He chuckled and gently lifted my chin, kissing me chastely. "I don't mind one bit. You know what's better than getting to do all that for the first time with you? It's getting to do it all for the first time again."

This time I slid my hand along his jaw and brought his mouth to mine. He tasted like a long-lost summer day, something I was so very familiar with but couldn't exactly recall. He was strong and warm, and he felt so right. "Okay," I said, breathless. "I need to sit down."

The concern was back. "Do you feel okay?"

"I feel great," I said as he helped me back to the couch. "But it's been a helluva morning and I'm kinda beat."

The tiredness was the worst part. Well, probably not the worst part—there were a lot of worst parts. But I never knew bone-tired was actually a real thing, but damn . . .

When I was reclined and comfy, he pulled his shirt

175

back on. He laughed at my pout. "I'll come back up and check on you in a bit."

I nodded. "Okay."

He sat down beside me and took my hand. He lifted my knuckles to his lips. "You remembering my tattoos means so much to me. If you remember nothing else, I won't mind. But you remembered this, and that's all I need."

"I just remember how it made me feel," I told him. "When I woke up, I didn't know what or where home was, except those wings kept coming back to me. They felt familiar when nothing else did. Like home."

His eyes were glassy and he put my palm to his cheek and let out a shaky breath. "Thank you."

"You okay?"

He nodded and laughed at himself, blinking back his tears. "I'm gonna let you get some rest, and I'm gonna plan the best first date ever for tonight."

I hummed out a sigh. "Our first date." Then I corrected. "Sorry, our second first date? Our first date all over again? I don't know what to call it. My brain gets slow when I'm tired."

He leaned down and kissed my forehead. "I know, baby. Get some rest. I'll just be downstairs. Call me if you need me."

I smiled and it took a second for his words to process. "Like it how you call me baby. And I like second first dates."

His smiling face was the last thing I remembered seeing before sleep stole me again. I stored it away in my mind, in my heart. I never wanted to forget him again. I finally had a piece of the puzzle. Just one single piece, but what a piece it was. That piece was Dallas. No, I didn't have any old memories of him, but I liked the new ones. Was I mad that those memories were stolen from me? Sure. Probably more sad than mad. But I couldn't do a damn thing about it. There was no point in expending energy I didn't have on things I couldn't fix.

And anyway, I looked forward to making more memories. New experiences. New memories.

Starting now. Starting new.

ABOUT THE AUTHOR

N.R. Walker is an Australian author, who loves her genre of gay romance. She loves writing and spends far too much time doing it, but wouldn't have it any other way.

She is many things: a mother, a wife, a sister, a writer. She has pretty, pretty boys who live in her head, who don't let her sleep at night unless she gives them life with words.

She likes it when they do dirty, dirty things... but likes it even more when they fall in love.

She used to think having people in her head talking to her was weird, until one day she happened across other writers who told her it was normal.

She's been writing ever since...

ALSO BY N.R. WALKER

Blind Faith

Through These Eyes (Blind Faith #2)

Blindside: Mark's Story (Blind Faith #3)

Ten in the Bin

Gay Sex Club Stories 1

Gay Sex Club Stories 2

Point of No Return – Turning Point #1

Breaking Point – Turning Point #2

Starting Point – Turning Point #3

Element of Retrofit – Thomas Elkin Series #1

Clarity of Lines – Thomas Elkin Series #2

Sense of Place – Thomas Elkin Series #3

Taxes and TARDIS

Three's Company

Red Dirt Heart

Red Dirt Heart 2

Red Dirt Heart 3

Red Dirt Heart 4

Red Dirt Christmas

Cronin's Key

Cronin's Key II

Cronin's Key III

Cronin's Key IV - Kennard's Story

Exchange of Hearts

The Spencer Cohen Series, Book One

The Spencer Cohen Series, Book Two

The Spencer Cohen Series, Book Three

The Spencer Cohen Series, Yanni's Story

Blood & Milk

The Weight Of It All

A Very Henry Christmas (The Weight of It All 1.5)

Perfect Catch

Switched

Imago

Imagines

Red Dirt Heart Imago

On Davis Row

Finders Keepers

Evolved

Galaxies and Oceans

Private Charter

Nova Praetorian

A Soldier's Wish

Upside Down

The Hate You Drink

Sir

Tallowwood

Reindeer Games

The Dichotomy of Angels

Throwing Hearts

Titles in Audio:

Cronin's Key

Cronin's Key II

Cronin's Key III

Red Dirt Heart

Red Dirt Heart 2

Red Dirt Heart 3

Red Dirt Heart 4

The Weight Of It All

Switched

Point of No Return

Breaking Point

Starting Point

Spencer Cohen Book One

Spencer Cohen Book Two

Spencer Cohen Book Three

Yanni's Story

On Davis Row

Evolved

Elements of Retrofit

Clarity of Lines

Sense of Place

Blind Faith

Through These Eyes

Blindside

Finders Keepers

Galaxies and Oceans

Nova Praetorian

Upside Down

Tallowwood

Free Reads:

Sixty Five Hours

Learning to Feel

His Grandfather's Watch (And The Story of Billy and Hale)

The Twelfth of Never (Blind Faith 3.5)

Twelve Days of Christmas (Sixty Five Hours Christmas)

Best of Both Worlds

Translated Titles:

Fiducia Cieca (Italian translation of Blind Faith)

Attraverso Questi Occhi (Italian translation of Through These Eyes)

Preso alla Sprovvista (Italian translation of Blindside)

Il giorno del Mai (Italian translation of Blind Faith 3.5)

Cuore di Terra Rossa (Italian translation of Red Dirt Heart)

Cuore di Terra Rossa 2 (Italian translation of Red Dirt Heart 2)

Cuore di Terra Rossa 3 (Italian translation of Red Dirt Heart 3)

Cuore di Terra Rossa 4 (Italian translation of Red Dirt Heart 4)

Natale di terra rossa (Red dirt Christmas)

Intervento di Retrofit (Italian translation of Elements of Retrofit)

A Chiare Linee (Italian translation of Clarity of Lines)

Spencer Cohen 1 Serie: Spencer Cohen

Spencer Cohen 2 Serie: Spencer Cohen

Spencer Cohen 3 Serie: Spencer Cohen

Spencer Cohen 4 Serie: Yanni's Story

Punto di non Ritorno (Italian translation of Point of No Return)

Punto di Rottura (Italian translation of Breaking Point)

Imago (Italian translation of Imago)

Il desiderio di un soldato (Italian translation of A Soldier's Wish)

Confiance Aveugle (French translation of Blind Faith)

A travers ces yeux: Confiance Aveugle 2 (French translation of Through These Eyes)

Aveugle: Confiance Aveugle 3 (French translation of Blindside)

À Jamais (French translation of Blind Faith 3.5)

Cronin's Key (French translation)

Cronin's Key II (French translation)

Au Coeur de Sutton Station (French translation of Red Dirt Heart)

Partir ou rester (French translation of Red Dirt Heart 2)

Faire Face (French translation of Red Dirt Heart 3)

Trouver sa Place (French translation of Red Dirt Heart 4)

Rote Erde (German translation of Red Dirt Heart)

Rote Erde 2 (German translation of Red Dirt Heart 2)

Vier Pfoten und ein bisschen Zufall (German translation of Finders Keepers)

Ein Kleines bisschen Versuchung (German translation of The Weight of It All)

Weil Leibe uns immer Bliebt (German translation of Switched)

Drei Herzen eine Leibe (German translation of Three's Company)

Sixty Five Hours (Thai translation)

Finders Keepers (Thai translation)